THE other AMERICA

Teens with CANCER

by Gail B. Stewart

Photographs by
Carl Franzén

Lucent Books, P.O. Box 289011, San Diego, CA 92198-9011

These and other titles are included in *The Other America* series:

Battered Women
Gangs
Gay and Lesbian Youth
Homeless Teens
Illegal Immigrants
People with AIDS
Teen Addicts
Teen Alcoholics

Teen Dropouts
Teen Fathers
Teen Mothers
Teen Runaways
Teens in Prison
Teens and Violence
Teens with Disabilities
Teens with Eating Disorders

Cover design: Carl Franzén

Library of Congress Cataloging-in-Publication Data

Stewart, Gail, 1949–
  Teens with cancer / by Gail B. Stewart
    p. ; cm. — (The Other America series)
Includes bibliographical references and index.
Summary: Discusses the stories of four young cancer patients and how each
handles the daily demands of family, education, social life, doctor visits, and
medical treatments and how each finds the strength and courage to continue
their battle against cancer.
  ISBN 1-56006-884-1 (hardcover : alk. paper)
  1. Tumors in children—Patients—United States—Biography. [1. Cancer—
Patients. 2. Diseases.]
  [DNLM: 1. Neoplasms—Adolescence—Juvenile Literature. QZ 201 S849t
2001] I. Title
  RC281.C4 S79 2002
  362.1'96994'00835—dc21

                                    2001001445

The opinions of and stories told by the people in this book are entirely their
own. The author has presented their accounts in their own words and has not
verified their accuracy. Thus, the author can make no claim as to the objectiv-
ity of their accounts.

Printed in the U.S.A.
Copyright © 2002 by Lucent Books, Inc.
P.O. Box 289011, San Diego, CA 92198-9011

Contents

Foreword

O, YES,
I SAY IT PLAIN,
AMERICA NEVER WAS AMERICA TO ME.
AND YET I SWEAR THIS OATH—
AMERICA WILL BE!

LANGSTON HUGHES

Perhaps more than any other nation in the world, the United States represents an ideal to many people. The ideal of equality—of opportunity, of legal rights, of protection against discrimination and oppression. To a certain extent, this image has proven accurate. But beneath this ideal lies a less idealistic fact—many segments of our society do not feel included in this vision of America.

They are the outsiders—the homeless, the elderly, people with AIDS, teenage mothers, gang members, prisoners, and countless others. When politicians and the media discuss society's ills, the members of these groups are defined as what's wrong with America; they are the people who need fixing, who need help, or increasingly, who need to take more responsibility. And as these people become society's fix-it problem, they lose all identity as individuals and become part of an anonymous group. In the media and in our minds these groups are identified by condition—a disease, crime, morality, poverty. Their condition becomes their identity, and once this occurs, in the eyes of society, they lose their humanity.

The Other America series reveals the members of these groups as individuals. Through in-depth interviews, each person tells his or her unique story. At times these stories are painful, revealing individuals who are struggling to maintain their integrity, their humanity, their lives, in the face of fear, loss, and economic and spiritual hardship. At other times, their tales are exasperating,

4

demonstrating a litany of poor choices, shortsighted thinking, and self-gratification. Nevertheless, their identities remain distinct, their personalities diverse.

As we listen to the people of *The Other America* series describe their experiences, they cease to be stereotypically defined and become tangible, individual. In the process, we may begin to understand more profoundly and think more critically about society's problems. When politicians debate, for example, whether the homeless problem is due to a poor economy or lack of initiative, it will help to read the words of the homeless. Perhaps then we can see the issue more clearly. The family who finds itself temporarily homeless because it has always been one paycheck from poverty is not the same as the mother of six who has been chronically chemically dependent. These people's circumstances are not all of one kind, and perhaps we, after all, are not so very different from them. Before we can act to solve the problems of the Other America, we must be willing to look down their path, to see their faces. And perhaps in doing so, we may find a piece of ourselves as well.

Introduction

Talli insists that it ranks as one of the major coincidences ever—and she may be right. The Wisconsin teen was doing a report three years ago on hockey legend Mario Lemieux for a school project.

"My father and I have been watching hockey ever since I was little," says Talli. "And I got interested in Lemieux, not only because he was such a great player, but because he'd gotten a kind of cancer called Hodgkin's disease—and he beat it."

The coincidence, says Talli, is that less than two months after finishing her report, she herself was diagnosed with Hodgkin's disease. While the news was grim, Talli, who turned seventeen this year, now considers herself lucky. After a long regimen of chemotherapy—taking strong medicines to kill any remaining cancer cells left in her body—Talli is today cancer-free. An active high school student, she skates on her school girls' hockey team.

"I've made a comeback like Mario," she says and laughs. "I wish I could score as many goals as he does, though!"

NOT ALONE

It oftens surprises people to hear that teenagers have cancer; it is usually thought of as an adult disease. However, medical authorities say that cancer is becoming more common than ever in young people. The National Childhood Cancer Foundation estimates that 1 in 330 Americans develops cancer before reaching the age of nineteen.

More than eleven thousand new cases of cancer in young people are diagnosed every year, but that number is growing. In fact, there is a 1 percent increase in childhood and teen cancer every year. The fifteen-to-nineteen age group has a higher rate of new cancer—double that of younger children.

The fact that there are many teens who are facing cancer is not surprising to Becky, an eighteen-year-old whose brother Tom was diagnosed with a cancerous brain tumor. She remembers how startled she was the first time she went to see him in the hospital.

"The elevator door opened on the twelfth floor," she says, "and I couldn't believe it—there were so many kids! Some were in the first stages of their treatment; others were near the last parts. Lots of little IV carts, lots of kids losing their hair from chemo. I think it made it easier for Tom, knowing there were kids that were in the same position he was. He wasn't alone, that's for sure."

MANY DISEASES

Many teens have no real knowledge about cancer until they or someone they know is diagnosed. Cancer is actually not a single disease, but many different diseases. Today medical researchers say over one hundred different types of diseases are known as cancer. However, all of these diseases have some things in common.

Most important, cancer involves the rapid growth of cells. Normally cells throughout the human body grow and divide over a length of time until they die. However, cancer cells keep growing and dividing in an uncontrolled way. Sometimes particular cells gather in one place and form a growth called a tumor. Over time a tumor can destroy normal tissue, making a person very sick.

No one is certain yet why cells suddenly behave this way in some people but not in others. In some cases, the tendency to develop a particular kind of cancer may be genetic. If a woman's mother had breast cancer, for example, that woman's daughters are slightly more at risk to develop the disease.

In other cases, the development of cancerous cells is triggered by some factor in one's lifestyle, such as smoking cigarettes. Cancer can also be triggered by the exposure to certain materials such as asbestos or toxic chemicals. By limiting their exposure to these triggers, people can significantly reduce their risk of many types of cancers.

TEEN CANCER—MORE RISKY?

But while these findings are important, they do not seem to pertain to teenagers and children with cancer. Cancers they are most likely to develop are *not* those most common in adults—those of the breast, prostate, lung, or colon. Young people diagnosed with cancer are most likely to have cancer of the white blood cells, bone, lymphatic system, or a cancerous tumor of the kidney, brain, or muscles. Unlike the predominantly "adult" cancers, the triggers of these cancers are largely a mystery to researchers.

"It doesn't mean these cancers can't be affected by triggers in the environment or the genetic background of a child or teenager," says one doctor. "But most of the known causes of adult cancers develop over a long time—for instance, a fifty-five-year-old man who has smoked since he was a teenager. But it is unlikely to find an environmental or lifestyle trigger that can explain a cancerous tumor in a baby's kidney. It's not the same thing."

Without knowing the causes of these cancers, health officials can do little to prevent them. But there are other ways in which teens and children with cancer are more at risk than adults. Diagnosing their cancers is more difficult, too, for their symptoms rarely seem to point to a serious problem.

"I FELT SO GUILTY"

One woman says that it took nearly six months for her son to be diagnosed with leukemia, or cancer of the white blood cells. He had a bad cold and an ear infection, but it seemed very similar to other viruses he'd had before.

"It's not the first thing doctors look for," she says. "His dad and I knew something was wrong—we could tell he was feeling lousy. But so many things could have explained the way he felt. Doctors thought a virus, then mono, then they thought he was anemic.

"We'd go in for checkups, and tests, and more tests. We'd see different doctors, too. And it wasn't for lack of trying—they tried almost everything. But leukemia wasn't near the top of their list, so it wasn't something they really checked for—not until everything else had been tried."

Another parent agrees. She says that her daughter's bone cancer went untreated for months; doctors reassured her that the pain her daughter felt in her leg was a muscle pull or perhaps growing pains.

"I felt so guilty for so long," she says. "After the diagnosis, I'd look back on how we put hot packs on the leg and gave her Advil. Obviously, neither the doctors nor I was on the right page."

Partly because of the difficulty of quick diagnosis and because of the nature of these cancers, they are more likely to be at a more advanced stage than cancers in adults. In fact, while about 20 percent of adult cancers have spread to another part of the body when they are diagnosed, 80 percent of teen and child cancers have spread. That makes the treatment even more difficult.

BEING TREATED

Young people's cancers are treated in much the same way as adults' cancers. Chemotherapy is a combination of strong medicines that are given intravenously. Chemotherapy, or "chemo," is usually done in a hospital over weeks or months. At first the teen may stay in the hospital until the first round of chemo is completed. After that she may take chemo as an outpatient, going back and forth between home and the hospital.

Chemotherapy is so powerful that it kills the cancer cells; however, it also kills many healthy cells. For that reason, it is not unusual for teens on chemo to be more susceptible to germs and viruses than other teens. Chemotherapy has other side effects, too—among them nausea, fatigue, and hair loss. At the end of the chemotherapy, hair will grow back and the other side effects will go away.

Surgery is necessary when there is a tumor, as in the case of bone cancer. Frequently teens with a cancerous tumor undergo chemotherapy first to shrink the tumor. After that surgeons remove it, along with some healthy tissue near the site of the tumor. It is important for doctors to make sure that no cancerous cells remain to spread to other tissue. In some instances, powerful X rays or high-energy electrons are used to kill cancer cells or tumors. This method of treatment is called radiation and is often used in combination with surgery, chemotherapy, or both.

"MIRACLES HAPPENING EVERY DAY"

Teens and children are often at a disadvantage in the diagnosis and prevention aspects of cancer, but the treatment of many of their cancers has improved a great deal in the past ten years.

"Some of these cancers were so serious that the diagnosis was virtually a death sentence ten or fifteen years ago," says one health worker. "And others, like osteosarcoma [bone cancer], were a guaranteed amputation. But those things are changing. More than 70 percent of teenagers and other kids with cancer are surviving now, achieving that status of being cured."

Most of the credit seems to go to a new branch of medicine that did not exist in years gone by—pediatric oncology. An oncologist is a doctor who specializes in the treatment of cancer, but paired with pediatrics—the knowledge of children's medicine—the combination is powerful.

Pediatric oncologists are usually connected with a children's hospital where cancer research is ongoing. That means that teens and younger children may take advantage of treatment ideas that are brand-new. For many teens at such hospitals, these cutting-edge treatments have meant the difference between life and death. More than 200,000 teens and younger children in the United States have survived because they participated in the clinical tests of promising new medicines—or known medicines used in new ways.

"This is a good example of when it's good to be a kid," says one doctor. "Most fifteen-year-olds are busy trying to be treated like adults, but if you're a fifteen-year-old with cancer, we tell you to be a kid until your cancer's gone. The care and treatment available to young cancer patients in the form of these clinical trials at children's hospitals is amazing. They're getting better; there are miracles happening every day."

OTHER CHALLENGES

However, while the treatments are achieving more and more success, teens with cancer say that they hate other aspects of the disease. Many find the loss of their hair—even though it is temporary—to be difficult. Others say they feel isolated from their friends and activities at school.

"I miss a lot of stuff," says Jared, seventeen. "I was supposed to be starting on the football team this year, and I never even made one practice. I got diagnosed over the summer, and I've been in the hospital six weeks. My friends come to see me, but it isn't the same at all. They just stand here, and I know they're uncomfortable."

While cancer is a hard battle for anyone, teens are at an especially difficult stage of life to experience the effects of the disease. "You're talking about drugs that make them lose their hair, or gain wait, or retain water, or get rashes," says one counselor. "And in the meantime, they are separated from their friends for long periods of time. They miss school—as well as all the activities that go with school. And all of this at a time in their lives when friends mean everything, when appearance seems so completely important. It's tough, and I am constantly amazed by how they get through it."

FOUR STORIES

The four young people whose stories make up this book are in various stages of this struggle. LaNé, twelve, was diagnosed with bone cancer when she was eight. Having completed chemotherapy and having had two surgeries on her leg, she today considers herself a typical teenager. Kristin, fifteen, was told by her doctor that he wouldn't be able to cure her of Hodgkin's disease, a cancer of the lymphatic system. "If a miracle is going to happen," he said, "it isn't going to happen here." Unwilling to give up, Kristin and her family today are one thouand miles from home, living in a Ronald McDonald House while she participates in a clinical trial that she hopes will make the difference for her. Cullen, eighteen, missed his freshman year of high school while going through treatment for leukemia. Although he is an active college freshman, he says he still hasn't regained the stamina he had before he got sick. Finally, Daniel, fifteen, is in the final stages of his chemotherapy. He is enjoying his first year of high school and would like to be a pediatric oncologist himself someday.

The stories of these four teenagers vary, but a current of strength runs through each one. They are honest in their explanations of their diagnosis and treatment and about some of the difficulties and frustrations that have been a part of their battle against cancer. And at the same time, they are aware that they have emerged as much different people than they were before.

LaNé

"I ALWAYS LOVED MY MOM AND MY GRANDPARENTS AND COUSINS AND EVERYBODY—BUT I KNOW HOW IMPORTANT THEY ARE NOW."

Diagnosed with bone cancer at the age of eight, LaNé has now been cancer-free for four years. She has stretched the limits of what her doctors believed she could accomplish.

The house is far out in the country, past the little Swedish town, past the little strip mall and the feed store, past the farms and the horse barns. The January wind is raw and strong and seems to be gathering momentum as it sweeps across the open fields near LaNé's house.

LaNé is just getting off the school bus, and we walk inside together. Her mother Kim waits by the door and smiles a welcome. She gets a snack for LaNé while we sit by an immense window looking out over a frozen lake.

"It doesn't look much like a lake now," says Kim. "But people catch lots of fish in there, I guess. It's a great view—lots of birds and everything. We're lucky to be able to stay here, that's for sure."

The house is not theirs, she explains. Kim's parents live here and have offered to let their daughter and granddaughter stay here, too. LaNé, drinking a glass of juice, smiles shyly.

"My grandma and grandpa have been really good about helping us out since I've been sick. So the four of us live here now."

OSTEOSARCOMA

LaNé (a combination of her mother's and father's last names, she explains) is twelve and a half. She's had cancer, although she is cancer-free now. And though she admits it scares her sometimes, she is fairly comfortable talking about it.

"If," she says, "my mom can stay and talk, too. Some of the stuff I don't know—I was only eight when it happened."

That said, LaNé looks to her mother to begin. Kim smiles at her daughter.

"Well, it was bone cancer LaNé had. It's called osteosarcoma, which is the clinical name. And when she was eight, she started complaining about her leg hurting her. I'd like to say that I had a suspicion that something was wrong, or a mother's intuition or something. But I didn't. LaNé had always been healthy, and I just figured it was something little, something easy to fix.

"Lots of times kids will have growing pains, you know. Like aches and pains that come and go. And I did what lots of mothers do—I asked other mothers. And people would say, 'Oh, sure, my son had that,' or, 'My daughter is going through that right now.' And I got ideas of what to do—a little aspirin or maybe a glass of milk right before bed."

Now twelve and a half years old, LaNé is free of the cancer she was diagnosed with when she was eight.

"Nothing Helped"

LaNé says that she remembers going to the doctor's office a lot that year.

"I guess the stuff my mom's friends told her didn't help much," she says. "Because it still hurt all the time. It was in the top part of my leg, the bone above the knee. That's the femur. And so we went to the clinic, here in town."

Kim nods. "They told me to try different things, too. Hot packs, cold packs. They sent me home with a sports bandage to put on her leg. I think that was the theory that what she had was a pulled muscle. But nothing seemed to do any good. But still, I wasn't worried.

"The thing about doctors—at least for most people—is that you believe them. You listen to them, because they seem to know what they're talking about. And they weren't worried. If anything, I'd get the idea that they were wondering why I was making such a big deal about it. They'd look at LaNé, have her walk for them, and they'd just shrug. 'Have her take some Advil' is what they suggested."

A Different Opinion

After almost four months, Kim says, the pain in her daughter's leg was more persistent than ever. More trips to the doctor had been pointless.

"I don't mean to be critical," she explains. "I mean, nine times out of ten, I'm sure that pain like this *is* nothing at all. But in this case, they were wrong.

"We ended up going to a different doctor—and she had different advice, too. She told me to take LaNé to an orthopedic specialist in town. And that's what started the whole thing in motion. The orthopedic specialist took an X ray right away."

Kim sighs. "See, if they'd taken one way back when, the first time I'd brought her to the clinic, they'd have found the lump. They could have seen it there in the bone. But anyway, the specialist saw it, and he urged me to see a specialist at the university, in the city."

Did she know it was cancerous? Kim shakes her head emphatically. "Not at all," she says. "Not at all. He didn't even know it was a tumor—he just saw some mass in the bone. It might be a tumor or an infection, he said. And I know this sounds funny, but I didn't even think cancer—even when he said the word 'tumor.' I guess when I think of cancer, I don't think of bones."

She looks at LaNé. "And not little eight-year-old girls."

Accompanied by her mother, LaNé waits in her doctor's office during a scheduled visit.

"THERE WAS NO DELAY"

LaNé says that the specialist they saw in the city did something she didn't expect at all—he put her leg in a cast.

"It was a really big cast, too," she says. "It was hard, like a plaster cast. It went all the way around my waist—it was way bigger than the kind of cast you usually see on someone with a broken leg."

Kim nods. "The doctor took one look at her X ray and put that cast on her. Then it was right into the hospital—no fooling around. And he didn't even know yet whether it was cancer. But he did know it was a tumor of some sort—I mean, all tumors aren't malignant. Some just grow, I guess.

"But whether it was cancer or not, the tumor was endangering her leg. It was putting so much pressure on her femur—pressure from the inside of the bone—that the bone could have shattered at any minute. Any fall, or hard bump, or anything. She could have broken her leg badly."

LaNé interrupts. "It wouldn't have been like a normal broken leg, either. That's why they worried. Because my bone would have shattered—broken into lots of parts. Something like that would have been almost impossible to heal. So that's why the cast was important."

MAKING A PLAN

The doctor told LaNé and her mother that he would need to do a biopsy before he knew for certain that the tumor was cancerous. But even before that, it was important that they shrink the tumor.

Visiting the doctor has become a routine experience for LaNé, who has been seeing her doctors regularly for the last four years.

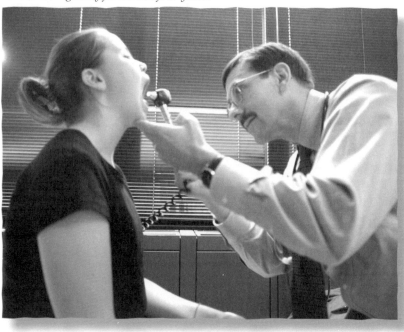

No matter what, it would have to be removed—and by using strong medicine, they could make it smaller.

"I wasn't really afraid," says LaNé. "I was eight, you know, and it wasn't really registering that it was a big deal. I guess I figured that my mom wasn't worried—she didn't cry or look sad. So I knew I would be all right."

Kim smiles. "It wasn't an act—I mean, I guess if I'd had time to think about it, I would have been scared. But the truth is, I was so busy talking to doctors, talking to family, being with LaNé, that I didn't allow myself to drift like that. So that turned out well, then—that she wasn't scared.

"The plan, then, was to use the chemo at first to shrink the thing and then take it out. So right away, she's in the hospital. They don't want to monkey around—the sooner they start treating it, if it's cancer, the better chance you have of beating it, you know? So it was a lot of activity really fast.

"The tumor was a slow-growing one—there was really no way of knowing how long it had been in there. They said, too, that it was pretty uncommon in a kid her age; usually it was teenagers who were diagnosed with this. It's funny how I get more scared now, thinking about what if I hadn't gone in that next day, or what would have happened if we just took the other doctors' advice and let it ride? That's scary, in hindsight."

A BIOPSY AND A PREDICTION

Kim knows now that the doctor suspected the tumor was cancerous, even though he wouldn't know until it was tested.

"I think just by the way it looked on the X ray," she says. "And most instances of this kind of cancer happen in kids' bones that are right around the knee. So when he did the biopsy and the tumor was cancerous, he wasn't surprised."

"They gave us a new doctor then, too," adds LaNé. "An oncologist—that's someone who specializes in cancer."

"Right," says Kim. "And they were pretty optimistic, which was really good. I mean, you hear 'cancer' and your world starts to tip, and the doctors know that. They know it's important to be clear about things, so you don't go off the deep end.

"So they told us that osteosarcoma, which is what she has, is much more treatable than it used to be. Ten years ago, they said, there was no choice but to amputate the leg. But they had come a long way, and the survival rate has really improved. More than 70 percent of kids recover from this, which is wonderful to hear. I mean, it would be more wonderful to hear that it wasn't cancer in the first place, but at least her odds were really, really good."

LOTS OF CHEMO

The treatment, they said, would be uncomfortable and lengthy.

It would consist of forty-two weeks of chemotherapy—that was to shrink the tumor. After that they would remove it and surgically insert a rod in her femur.

"That was to keep it strong," says LaNé. "It's just that when they take out bone—which they had to do, to get at the whole tumor—your leg isn't as strong. So the rod would help.

"Anyway, I probably didn't even hear them when they talked about the forty-two weeks. Or maybe I just didn't know what that was going to be like—chemo. I'd never heard of it, being eight. But it went on forever, it seemed like. And I felt sick all the time. That's what I think of most about that time, just feeling sick.

"I was in the hospital two weeks that first time. You don't have to stay in the hospital the whole time, the whole forty-two weeks— that would have really been horrible!"

Kim agrees. "It was quite a drive from where we lived back then. And there is a Ronald McDonald House right near that hospital, but we were just a few miles shy of being eligible to stay there. But, gee, I don't know. I think I would have felt guilty. I had to look at it like this—there are a limited number of rooms there, and there are families from all over the country that have come here. Why should I be taking up that space and a family from far away really needs it?

"I admit, there were some days when I'd be making that long drive, and I'd wish we were staying there. But I'd feel like I was taking one of their rooms. I felt like we were pretty lucky to live near a place with so many medical facilities. Plus, we were especially lucky to have so many family members around. That helped so much—LaNé had grandparents, cousins, aunts, and uncles. And me," she says with a laugh.

"Almost every night she was there, I'd stay in the room with her. There were a couple of nights that my parents would give me a break—they'd stay with her. You know, the nurses were absolutely great, but they have so many kids to take care of. I just felt like LaNé was so little and so sick. I just couldn't have left her there on her own—I wouldn't have felt right."

TROUBLE FROM A HANGNAIL

After spending the first two weeks in the hospital, LaNé and her mother went home for short times—usually on weekends.

"The chemo I had was five days, and then we'd get two days off," LaNé says. "As long as my blood and everything was OK, they'd let me stay at home. There was a nurse who came to our house and checked that.

"But anytime there was any kind of infection or anything, I'd have to go back to the hospital, just to be safe. They'd always tell us how any little germ can do more damage to someone on chemo. Little kids with cancer don't have anything to fight off infections like healthy kids do."

Did she ever get an infection and have to return to the hospital for an unscheduled stay? She nods.

"I had to go back because of a hangnail!" she says, laughing. "That's pretty hard to believe, I know. But it started out as a cuticle that got infected, just a hangnail. And it made me get sick! I remember that time, because I was in such a bad mood. Most of the time I'd try to be nice and polite and everything. But the nurses were moving me from one bed to another, and my leg hurt while they were doing that. And I started yelling."

She giggles, looking quickly at her mother.

"Let's just say you've been *more* pleasant than you were that day," says Kim dryly. "Your voice really carried, and I think we were all a little surprised. But most of the time you were so patient. I guess everyone has to blow up sometimes. And it turned out OK; they put you on an antibiotic, and the infection went away."

HARD ON A MOTHER

Did Kim find herself getting depressed and angry herself? She shrugs, remembering.

"In a way, I felt bad," she says, choosing her words carefully. "I think most every mother would rather be sick or hurt herself than watch a child go through something like this. I'd just keep my fingers crossed those times when we could go home, hoping she wouldn't come down with something. They had a rule, you

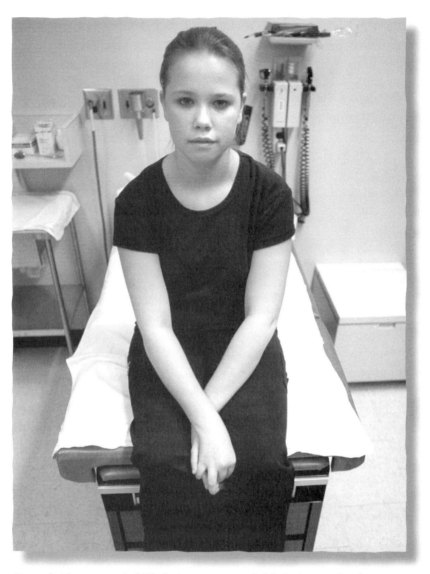

To combat her cancer, LaNé's doctors recommended forty-two weeks of chemotherapy and two surgeries on her leg.

know, that any fever—even one as low as 100.5—and you're right back in that hospital bed where they can keep an eye on you.

"And like LaNé says, it happened. Just when you think things are manageable, there's a fever, a little sniffles, or something. But still, I wasn't worrying. I had—and still have—an awful lot of confidence in those doctors and nurses. They really are accomplishing amazing things."

Keeping Herself Amused

It's one thing for an adult or older child to be confined to home or to a hospital bed for long periods of time, but quite another for an eight-year-old.

"I mostly remember sleeping," LaNé says. "I was tired, probably from the medicine. I'd get rashes from the chemotherapy, and then I'd get medicines to help the rash. Those would make me fall asleep. Sometimes I felt sick to my stomach. But there were times when my mom and I did stuff. We watched television a lot, and I had some presents—things to do. I had a bead set, and some other craft things.

"My grandparents came to visit a lot, and that was great! I learned to play rummy, and that was fun. Sometimes there was stuff going on in the hospital that would be fun, like they'd bring in dogs and let us pet them. Sometimes football players would come in, but I didn't know who they were. Some of the boys did, probably, or the older kids."

Kim says that children's wards are good about trying things to keep patients' spirits up. "I think it's so important for the kids to laugh sometimes, to forget about how they hurt. The puppies were great; the visitors were great. It just takes everyone's mind off their troubles—even if it's just for a few minutes during the afternoon. And then we'd have something to talk about—something to tell Grandma and Grandpa about when they came to visit."

Being at Home

When it became apparent that the treatment was going to take a long time, Kim knew things would have to change. She quit her job to be able to take care of LaNé, and they moved in with her parents.

"That was nice, but it was also a big change," she says. "We'd lived in a nice little town, and we had friends. LaNé's cousins had lived nearby, too. It was kind of a trade-off, because we saw more of the grandparents, which was great. But LaNé really misses seeing her cousins all the time, like she used to."

LaNé agrees. "My cousin Felicia is a little older than me, and she was especially good to have around when I lost my hair. I knew it was falling out—just clumps at a time. It would be on my clothes or my pillow—just like how a cat sheds, I guess. I didn't mind that much. Sometimes I'd pull it out myself—it would come out real easy. I'd even throw it at my grandpa, because he's always teasing me.

"But sometimes other people would stare. Not at the hospital— lots of kids are bald there. But when we'd go out, like to the store. And Felicia was great, because she'd see them staring at me or whispering. She'd just start saying things to them; she didn't care about scolding people."

Kim laughs. "She's got no trouble speaking her mind, that's true. She's very protective, especially of LaNé. That was good for LaNé, too—it made her realize that the discomfort was all in the minds of other people, not herself. But I knew that deep down inside, the staring hurt. Little kids, they don't have any sense about that. I'm sure they don't intend to be cruel, but it hurts all the same."

"She's Got a Lot of Hardware in There"

After her chemotherapy was completed, the doctors agreed that the tumor had shrunk enough to be removed. They took it out, along with half of her femur.

"The knee is a prosthesis," explains Kim. "It's not her own knee—but it works fine. And she's got a rod inside the bone, to support it. The rod is a special one that can be lengthened as she grows. She's got a lot of hardware in there, that's for sure.

"After the operation, we heard about all the things that LaNé wouldn't be able to do, because of the artificial knee and the rod. Some of the things are obvious, like playing rough contact sports like football—any activity where she has a risk of really hurting her leg. I mean, we all know that you can hurt your leg even without doing things like that, but I guess the odds are a lot better if you don't go out for the hockey team."

LaNé says she would rather think about the things she *can* do.

"I can swim and ride horses," she says. "I really like riding—my friend has two horses, and we go riding over at her place. And at school, in gym class, I do most of the stuff."

She looks guiltily at her mother. "I play what they're playing, usually. And it's worked out OK. They don't do anything really rough in gym class."

Kim closes her eyes, smiling. "I guess I don't need to hear this, right?"

A Setback

Although in the years since her chemotherapy and operation she has had no recurrence of the cancer, LaNé has suffered a different setback.

"I broke my leg—the one with the rod," she says. "I was pushing my friend on a swing, and I slipped in the mud. It fractured, and then I had to be back in that big cast again. It's called a spike cast, but I'm not sure why. My mom thinks that it's kind of shaped like a spike, because it goes around my waist at the top, and then down."

Kim interrupts. "But there'd already been a setback before that—it was a problem with the first rod they'd put in. It was sort of loose, and it was causing her pain—and that wasn't supposed to

LaNé roughhouses with a friend. Though she can participate in most activities, LaNé must be careful not to risk injuring her leg.

happen. So they did what's called a transfer, meaning that they put in a different rod. But something wasn't working right, because what's supposed to happen is that the bone tissue is supposed to knit together, to grow.

"So when they went in there to repair things after she broke her leg, that was sort of a blessing. Because now they say it's starting to generate its own bone, like it's supposed to. The femur will never grow back the way it was, but it will get stronger from the inside. So a blessing in disguise, I guess."

"THERE ARE SOME GOOD MEMORIES"

Obviously there were some negative aspects to her experience, says LaNé. She missed a lot of school, and that set her back. "I missed the end of third grade from April on," she says. "And then fourth grade was my chemo year—it was mostly spent in the hospital. My mom says she felt like she knew every inch of that place.

"So when I was ready to come back to school, I couldn't go on with my friends. But what happened was, that's when we moved here, to live with my grandparents. So in a way that was good, because it's all new kids. I mean, it would have felt weird to see my

Since moving away from her old neighborhood, LaNé has made new friends and is happy at her new school.

friends all in a class without me. But here, it's OK. It didn't seem like I was a grade behind—at least not to them."

Were there any good things during that time? LaNé nods.

"Disney World," she says. "We got to go there—my mom and me and my cousin Felicia, too."

"Make-A-Wish," explains Kim. "Because it was a life-threatening disease, Dot at the hospital gave us the forms to fill out, and it happened. It was really a great thing—we'd never been, and LaNé was so excited.

"She was uncomfortable a lot of the time—she wasn't completely done with chemo, and she had some bad mouth sores from the medicine. That made it hard to eat—just like when you have cold sores, you know? Things aggravate them, make them sting. But even with that, and even though she was tired, she had a great time. That was one of the real high points."

"IT CHANGES YOUR LIFE"

LaNé says that even though she's never wanted to go back to that time in her life, there are other good things that happened because of her bout with cancer. "I really had nice people taking care of me," she says. "My favorite nurses were Kathy, Kim, and Tammy. I liked them because they were kind—it seemed like they wanted me to get better. Not because it was their job. I can't even think how awful it would be for a kid to be going through chemo and everything without nurses like that!

"And it made me really appreciate how good my family is. I always loved my mom and my grandparents and cousins and everybody—but I know how important they are now."

Kim agrees. "This whole thing changes your life, no question about that. You spend more time with people you love, because it's instinctive. You have to—you need each other. And LaNé and I got really close, too—I guess we had to, since we spent every waking minute within a few feet of each other!

"I'll tell you something, though. You spend so much time just thinking about things: You wonder about why certain things happen to certain people—you know what I'm talking about? I used to think how unfair it was that an eight-year-old kid gets cancer—I mean, why her? She didn't deserve something like this!

"And then I realized one day that me thinking about whether it was fair or unfair is silly. In a way, then, I'm saying that if it shouldn't have happened to her, it should have happened to someone else. And that's wrong. No one's daughter or son or mother or father or whatever—no one should have to get it.

"I thought after a while that maybe LaNé got it for a reason, because maybe she had the strength somehow. I don't know where cancer comes from, and I don't think doctors know, either. But the strength is in her; she's got it. She handled some very tough times. I guess for me, that's a better way of looking at it—otherwise you could go crazy!"

COMPUTER, CHRISTINA AGUILERA, AND TALKING ON THE PHONE

Having recovered from cancer and her fractured leg, LaNé says life is very good these days. "I like school pretty well," she says. "The teachers are mostly OK. I did get a D in science last semester, and that wasn't good. My mom didn't get mad, but she says she knows I can do a lot better than that. I hope so—she's more confident than I am about it.

"I don't just have like one best friend; I have a bunch of friends that I like equally, I think. One of my friends had cancer, too—I forgot to say that. She had it in the bone in her arm, and they had to do some kind of bone marrow exchange or something. I think she's going to be OK—but that was a coincidence, finding that out.

"Anyway, I think I'm pretty much like other girls in my grade. I love playing on the computer—I visit the chat rooms, and that's fun. I talk on the phone to my friends. My mom says that maybe if I keep my room up, keep it really clean for a while, I can get a phone jack in my room, so I can have the phone in there.

"I like going to movies, and I have a CD player. My favorite singers right now are Christina Aguilera and—let's see." She thinks for a moment. "Oh, yeah, LeAnn Rimes. I *do not* like boy bands. I'm not into Backstreet Boys or N'Sync, but some of my friends are."

THE CONTEST

The most exciting thing that's happened in a while is winning first prize in a contest she'd forgotten that she entered. "It was so weird," says LaNé, talking excitedly. "I drew this picture for a contest they had at the hospital. I mean, I had drawn it back almost a

Like many kids her age, LaNé enjoys playing on the computer and listening to music.

year ago—and they sent me this letter saying that I'd won. And the best part is my drawing was going to be used on a bunch of stuff for the Children's Cancer Research Fund."

Kim admits she'd forgotten about the contest, too. "There are so many things the hospital organizes for the kids, you sort of forget," she says. "But this was a really big honor—it's kind of like designing a stamp, you know? The Children's Cancer Research Fund—CCRF, people usually say—is a big deal. They do fund-raising for hospitals and research, and on everything they give out this year will be the picture LaNé drew—on calendars, on notecards, stationery, stuff like that."

LaNé points to the wall in the kitchen, where a framed picture of a butterfly hangs. "See, that's the picture, right there," she says proudly. "That's a butterfly, and back behind it is an angel. The butterfly is saying, 'And they shall be cured.' I spelled 'cured' wrong, but like I said, that was a whole year ago.

"Anyway, they asked me why the butterfly is saying that. I just liked the sound of it. I remember that I'd just finished watching the movie *Ace Ventura*, you know? And he said something like that in the movie. It stayed with me, I guess."

27

Kim says that the angel in the picture ties in with the CCRF, too. "It's kind of a sad story, but it's sweet," she says. "It was about twenty years ago, I think, that a little girl was saving for a bike. And she got cancer—and she realized after a while that she wasn't going to be around to finish saving for that bike. She told her parents to donate the money to help other kids with cancer. And I guess that's how the whole organization began. So it's really an honor, isn't it, getting chosen like that?"

"I Got to Wear a Formal"

Her prizewinning drawing was officially unveiled at the annual fund-raiser for the organization, which occurred a few months before.

"I got to meet Van and Cheryl—do you know who they are?" LaNé asks. "They're the DJs in the morning on KS95. And Van was one of the hosts at the fund-raiser. We have a whole bunch of pictures from that night.

"There was also a guy that sang, Bruce Hornsby. He's famous. And he signed the back of my picture! I got to wear a formal, sort of a shiny blue. And my main duty was to draw a number for someone to win a big prize—like a raffle. It was pretty successful, too—they raised more than a million dollars."

Did she feel shy, standing up in front of the room with all those adults? She smiles.

"Yeah, in a way. But the one thing that helped was I'd gone to the radio station a few days before, to meet Van and Cheryl. So it wasn't so strange and new that night, I guess. And he was really nice—he talked just regular, so I didn't get nervous. And people were very nice to me—it was OK."

Optimistic Doctors, Guilty Mother

With such optimism from LaNé's doctors, is there reason to be worried about her future?

"I take a lot of comfort in knowing that she isn't any more at risk for getting other kinds of cancer," says Kim. "Some cancers, you know, they leave you pretty vulnerable for getting different ones. So you never really feel like it's over. The only place they are concerned about is her lungs, though. I guess there's a link between bones and lungs.

"So we are careful about that. We go in every few months for a chest scan, to make sure no cancer cells have come back and are

hiding out in there. But she's been great—nothing is out of the or-
dinary. So I'm very, very optimistic."

That doesn't mean that she doesn't worry about things, Kim says.

"I think this is all backlash from five years ago," she says with a
laugh. "Now when she says she has a headache or something, I
worry. I think it's something—it means something. I had a lot of
guilt about that sore leg, feeling like I didn't do enough, and it's
coming back to haunt me now. Poor LaNé, she'll be thirty-five with
kids of her own, and I'll be worrying when she has an upset stomach or a headache."

*Even though she has been through more medical procedures than most kids her
age, LaNé considers herself a typical teenager.*

"Sometimes I Get Scared"

LaNé admits that she gets scared before her checkups with her doctor. "Sometimes I think it's coming back," she says. "I think about that when I'm in my room at night, before I fall asleep. I usually don't think that much about it, except the night before I go to the doctor. And then I get scared.

"But when we go to the doctor and he says that I'm fine, I get relieved. I forget about it for a while, and then before the next visit, you know, it happens again. I can't sleep at all when that happens. I wonder if other kids think that way, or am I the only one? I also wonder if I'm ever going to outgrow this."

Her mother nods sympathetically. "I know how you feel," she says. "And I bet that before too long, you'll get so used to being healthy, that you won't think about it. Sometimes I am amazed at how fast you've gotten well!

"The thing is," she says, "LaNé's done so much that they said she'd never be able to do. I mean, they told us she'd never run and walking would be very hard for her. Well, she's run, and she's even been on a bike, although I know she wasn't supposed to.

"But it's such a pleasure seeing her be confident, pushing herself. LaNé got cancer just when she was on the verge of really starting to enjoy some new sports. She had just started on a soccer team, and she'd always wanted to do gymnastics. So those things, too, were on the 'She'll never do' list. But who knows?" she says, smiling at her daughter.

"Yeah, who knows?" says LaNé, smiling. "Maybe I'll figure out a way to play soccer or something. Or maybe they'll invent something to make my leg even stronger in the future. Whatever happens, doctors shouldn't say 'never' to kids. That's like a dare that's hard to refuse!"

Kristin

"I'VE GOT A **30** PERCENT CHANCE
OF SURVIVING THIS. IT MAY
SOUND LOW TO YOU, BUT TO ME,
IT'S A LOT BETTER THAN ZERO."

Kristin has been fighting Hodgkin's disease with limited success. Six months ago, her doctors declared they could do no more for her; now she and her family are a long way from home, living in a Ronald McDonald House, hoping an experimental program can stop her cancer.

Kristin is sitting in the dining area of the house, a petite girl with wispy hair. Her face has the "chipmunk cheek" look that many of the children here have—a temporary side effect of the strict drug regimen they are undergoing. She is glad, she says, to be doing something different. Here at the Ronald McDonald House, a thousand miles from home, there is very little for a fifteen-year-old to do most of the time.

"IT'S HARD NOT BEING HOME"

"I don't mean to complain," Kristin says quickly. "This is a great place, and everything is clean and people are really friendly. And the idea that my whole family can stay here with me while I'm getting treatment—that's nice. I'm going to be here at least another month, and can you imagine how much a motel would cost for all that time? So I'm grateful. But you know, it's hard not being home."

Kristin, her parents, and her thirteen-year-old brother, Trey, have come to the Midwest from New Jersey. Her doctors there had told her that there was nothing they could do to stop the progress of the cancer in her system.

"My mom didn't want to accept that," she says simply. "None of us did, I guess. And she heard about this hospital here in Minneapolis that is doing a lot of new stuff, trying new things for cancer. So we sent all my hospital records, all the charts, to see if they'd let me come here and maybe have a shot at getting better. And—well," she concludes, giggling. "So here we are."

"I'D HAD SWOLLEN GLANDS BEFORE"

When did she first learn that she was sick? Kristin takes a deep breath and thinks for a moment.

"I had been sick with mono," she says. "And afterward I started to get a big lump on my neck. On the inside, you know? I'd had swollen glands before—I mean, everyone has. That's normal when you're sick—they kind of swell up because you're fighting an infection. But my lump was farther down, down by my collarbone. And I'd never had a swollen gland that was that far down.

"I told my mom and had her feel where the lump was. She wasn't worried, because she called the nurses' hot line. And they just said it was normal when you have mono. So we didn't think too much about it for a while. I figured it probably was what they said—I hadn't had mono before, so for all I knew, *everybody* got lumps there."

Kristin stops talking and waves to a tired-looking woman wheeling a stroller. The little boy in the stroller is bald and has a white face mask on.

"How's it going?" Kristin says, smiling. The mother shrugs and smiles back.

ONE TEAR

"Anyway," she continues, "I didn't worry about it. But then I developed congestion in my chest, you know, like when you have a bad cough and it's hard to breathe? So we went to the hospital on base—we live on a military base. And they took an X ray, and I guess they saw something that made them nervous. I know now that they suspected cancer. But they didn't tell me. I'm not sure if they told my parents or not."

The doctors at the base hospital did a biopsy, taking a small tissue sample of the lump in her neck. After examining it, they learned it was cancerous.

"We found out a week later," she remembers. "I remember the exact date—I mean, it would be pretty strange if I didn't, right? It was like the worst thing that had ever happened to me. But really, to tell the truth, I wasn't that scared when we went back to the doctor. When you're my age, you don't think about stuff being serious.

"Anyway, my whole family was there—my parents, Trey, and my sister, Erin—she's twenty-two. And the doctors just told us that what I had was Hodgkin's disease. I remember that when they said that, I wasn't sure if it was bad news or not. I hadn't ever heard of Hodgkin's disease. But my parents and my sister started crying. And then the doctors explained that it was a form of cancer. And I didn't cry as much as they did—I just had this one tear. That was it."

"I HATED THAT FEELING"

Kristin says that one of the worst parts about hearing that news wasn't the news itself, but the feeling she had of being powerless.

"It was like they were all sad and crying," she says. "Erin was so upset she ran out of the room. That worried me a lot—I kept thinking I should go out and find her. I just wanted to do *something!* I didn't want to sit there feeling bad. I wanted to get to the next part, where they tell us what to do, what the next step is. I didn't want to feel like—I don't know, like a victim. Or weak."

Kristin says she wasn't afraid when she was told she had cancer. "When you're my age, you don't think about stuff being serious."

33

She sighs, remembering. "Anyway, the doctors suggested we go to a children's hospital in Philadelphia. See, the base hospital wasn't equipped to take care of kids with cancer. This place in Philadelphia was supposed to specialize in that, so it made sense to go there."

A VERY SOCIAL TEENAGER

Kristin looks tired. She wants to keep talking, she insists, but she'd like to go up to her family's room on the third floor. The living area of the house is pleasant—like a small apartment building rather than a dormitory or hospital.

"You can tell which one's our door," she says, stepping off the elevator. "The one with all the Christmas decorations. We're going to be here through January, and we'd have lots of stuff up if we were home. So this seems like the best thing to do.

"What I was going to say before is one of the things that's hardest about being away from home is that I'm away from my friends. And if you knew me—I mean, before I got sick—you'd know that I was *very* social," she says, laughing. "My mom would really emphasize the 'very.'

"I guess I'm a pretty typical teenager—or I was. I wasn't ever home. I have lots of friends on the base, and we'd sleep over all the time. Oh, and I have to tell you that I did get in trouble once for that. We have this rule, where you have to check in every two hours—just to let my mom know where you are. But one time I'd been at a friend's house watching movies. And I sort of forgot.

"Anyway, something like five hours had gone by, and my mom called the police—the base police. I found that out as I was walking home, and I saw all these police officers looking in the windows of some of the empty houses on base. Like they were searching for something. I asked them what they were doing, and they said, 'We're looking for this girl, Kristin.' I'm like, 'Ooooh, that's me!' It all worked out OK; it's just that my mom is careful with us, and I was sort of a challenge, I guess."

TELLING MEGAN

Kristen remembers how funny she felt around her friends after finding out she had cancer. "I felt different," she says. "Right away, I thought, 'I'm not the same as you anymore.' I didn't say that, of course. And it only lasted a minute, feeling that. My best friend at

As a social teenager, Kristin finds it difficult living so far from her friends.

that time was Megan, and we'd made plans for her to come over that night. I didn't know if I really wanted to do anything, you know? But she came, and I just took a deep breath and told her.

"She thought I was just joking around at first, she's like, 'Yeah, right.' But then she realized I wasn't laughing, and she started crying. I guess that's when I really cried for the first time, too. But it was a shock to her—she hadn't even realized I was having tests done or anything. She just had figured that I'd been staying out of school because of the mono.

"Well, anyway, I told Megan that I was going to be fine. I needed to say that as much as she needed to hear it. I was in a really weird place then, because I didn't have the vaguest idea about cancer in kids my age, or Hodgkin's disease, or any of it. So I was just going on my usual thing of being optimistic. I figured things would turn out fine."

AN OPTIMISTIC PROGNOSIS

Kristin says she had very little time to think about her situation, for she was admitted to the hospital in Philadelphia the very next week.

"Right—I didn't have time to worry," she says with a shrug. "My family got busy right away, figuring out how everything would work—what my brother and sister were going to do, packing, all that stuff. As it turned out, all of us except my sister went down. She was still too upset, so she stayed.

"I was really glad to be doing something about it. That's the thing when you find out bad news like this—it's important to get busy. I mean, doing *anything* is better than sitting around thinking about it, right? So we met with the doctors there, and they ex-

Kristin's brother (right) and parents moved away from their home to be with Kristin during her treatment.

plained to us what they were going to do, how the routine worked, and about Hodgkin's.

"It was sort of reassuring that they had a routine—I mean, it wasn't something that was new and strange to them. They dealt with kids with cancer all the time. I liked knowing that they'd help me, too. They told me right away that I had a very good chance to beat the cancer. It's a real treatable kind—about 80 percent of the time it can be cured."

LESS OPTIMISTIC

The doctors had based their optimism on the X rays and test results provided to them by the base hospital. However, after doing their own exam, the doctors in Philadelphia found that Kristin's cancer had spread.

"I had a big mass on my chest," she says. "It hadn't been there before, but it was really big by the time I was in Philadelphia. I knew something was wrong, because I was having trouble breathing. Basically, the mass was crushing my lung—what the doctors called a 'collapsed lung.'"

Kristin smiles sadly. "So then they were all of a sudden less optimistic. They stopped telling me how I was going to be fine and about how all these other kids get better—that all stopped. They admitted me right away and started chemotherapy. My parents told me afterward that the doctors told them that if I hadn't started chemo right at that moment, I wouldn't have lived a week."

She adjusts a pillow on her bed and leans back against the wall. "That was a strange thing to hear, you know? It was spooky— that's the only way I can describe it. Scary and sad—I guess all of those things."

STARTING CHEMO

The first round of chemo was to last a week; she would stay in the hospital all during that time.

"It wasn't so terrible, not really," she says. "I was scared, because I'd heard all the buzz words about chemo—how you spend your whole time throwing up and watching your hair fall out. But I didn't really feel sick, other than having trouble breathing, like I said before.

"That was a relief, not getting sick to my stomach," Kristin says, grinning. "I absolutely *hate* throwing up; I mean, I can't stand even being near people who *might* throw up. I hate hearing someone in the next room throwing up! Really, I have to run out of the room if I think someone is going to. So when they said they had some medicine that would make me less likely to throw up, I was glad. And it worked.

"Actually, the chemo worked really fast that week, because the mass in my lung was going away. I could tell, because it was so much easier to breathe! So I passed my first round—I would come back for three days at a time after that for new rounds. And my mom and dad both came with me—and usually Trey, too. I think it was better for him and for me that we were all together."

THE HAIR GOES

Kristin runs a hand over her short hair and smiles ruefully.

"The hair part—not so good. I had long hair back then, way past my shoulders. I couldn't imagine losing it. And after that first week, I hadn't lost any yet, so I was hopeful. But then I went back for a second round, and it started falling out. I could see strands of it on my shirt all the time. I tried holding on to it as long as I could—I'd put it up in a bun, just having it flat on my head so the weight of it wouldn't pull it out. But no, it was a lost cause.

"It was coming out in clumps, getting all tangled. It was pretty awful. I finally gave up, and I had my mom cut it short. I got pretty choked up when she did that, I remember. It was kind of like I'd lost a fight. I know it wasn't that big a deal, not compared to having cancer. But it made me sad anyway. I didn't want short hair. But short hair would have been better than being bald.

"I stopped thinking about it after a while, though. When I'd go home between chemo sessions, my friends didn't treat me any different. My family didn't, of course. I know people looked at me when we'd go to the store or something; people I didn't know. But I didn't care. I figured it was their problem, I guess. My family says I have a tough exterior—and I guess I'm glad that they made me that way."

"IT WAS DISCOURAGING AFTER A WHILE"

Kristin says the doctors had found a number of tumors during the time she was at the hospital, but they would shrink after chemo. "I had one on my kidney, one on my spine, under my arm—and those would go away. The biggest one, the one on my chest? That

Hair loss is a common side effect of chemotherapy. Kristin admits that it bothered her at first but says, "I stopped thinking about it after a while."

disappeared completely. The doctors would do CAT scans, X rays, all kinds of tests, to make sure. The only one I have right now is on my chest wall.

"But anyway, these things would go away, but then in a while they'd come back again. Go away, come back. It looked like it was never going to end. I'd get so happy when the doctor would come in with the lab results and say, 'Well, the such-and-such is gone, and that's really good news.' But then later the thing would pop up somewhere else. It was so discouraging.

"The thing about a disease like this is that it takes a long time to fight it. And all that time, you get all focused on these little tiny things like blood counts, and levels of this and that, and numbers and percentages. It's really weird, in a way. It's like your world gets really little, and you just think about numbers of cells, or whatever. When your red blood count goes up, you get happy. When it goes down, you get scared. When the tumor is gone— well, you get happy for a while."

BAD TIMES

Kristin says that she had setbacks and she didn't feel well at all. "I had another one that popped up in my chest," she remembers. "I would like push my lung, and it started to weep—that's what they called it. Anyway, it was really hard for me to breathe, even little breaths. They had to drain fluid out of my lung, and that's really uncomfortable while it's happening. They put you on medicine first, and then they put a really long needle in your back.

"They drained lots—one time it was over a liter of fluid. No wonder it was hard to breathe, right? But then, you can breathe again, and you don't feel so sick anymore. Just tired."

Kristin sits patiently as a nurse draws blood, a routine procedure for cancer patients.

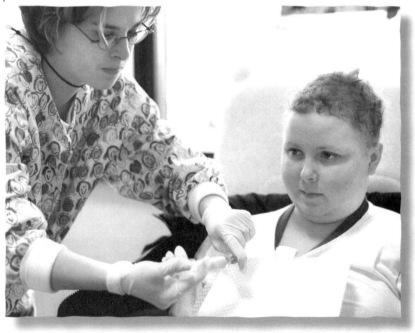

Kristin says the doctors weren't happy that the tumors would reappear and decided to change tactics. "They told me that they were going to give me a harder dose of chemo," she says. "So they gave me this new stuff, and they let me go home. I remember thinking, 'Boy, that wasn't bad. Maybe this is going to work.'"

"Ask the Doctor"

Kristin says that another setback soon followed.

"I started to develop another lump here, on my neck," she says, pointing to the right side of her throat. "The opposite side from that first one. It was small at first, but in four days it was as big as a softball. It was gross and huge.

"So, back to the hospital. The doctors said it was a fast-growing tumor. Duh!" she says, shaking her head. "And they were going to start me on radiation therapy, to zap it. So that's what I did. And that's when it all came down on me. I'd been really positive and optimistic, and strong, and everything. But I was so sick of it all!"

Kristin's eyes well up with tears, and she brushes them aside with the back of her hand. "I was thinking how much I hate it, going back and forth from home to here, to that stupid hospital. With the stupid doctors who said they could help me get well, and they didn't seem to know what to do. I didn't like feeling happy one minute and sad the next.

"Anyway, I was really feeling sorry for myself. I remember lying there, and my mom was next to me reading a magazine. I just looked at her and said, 'I'm not going to die from this, am I?' She told me she didn't know. She said, 'Ask the doctor.'"

"You Can't Keep Me Here"

The doctor wasn't there at the time, Kristin says, but the next time he came in, she asked him point-blank.

"I said it the same way, 'I'm not going to die from this, am I?' And he said, 'Yes, you are.' Just like that. He basically said they had no hope, and they were at the point of giving up. He said, 'If a miracle is going to happen, it isn't going to happen here.'

"I was really mad then. I mean, I'm not sure why I even asked; I hadn't asked before. I think it was just that everyone seemed so quiet; none of the doctors were ever smiling or acting confident. I guess I already knew, even before I asked. But I didn't like what he said. I started crying, and after a while I just stared off into space for a really long time."

Kristin is comforted by her mother, who has helped her deal with the emotional toll of her disease.

Kristin says that although they had no hope of making her better, they still wanted to keep her in the hospital awhile longer, because she'd started running a temperature.

"I told him I had a temperature because I was upset," she says. "I told him that I get overworked when I get mad and sad at the same time—that was the reason. It wasn't the cancer. It wasn't the medicine. It wasn't the radiation, either. I said, 'No, the other doctor just told me I'm going to die, so you can't keep me here. I'm going home to tell my brother and sister. So I'm leaving, since you're giving up on me.'"

Kristin sighs. "So they sent me home."

THE BEARER OF BAD NEWS

She says that was the worst thing—having to tell her brother and sister such frightening news. "Trey was there when we came home," she says, "but my sister wasn't. I'd wanted to tell them at the same time. But I told one of my friends, and then I started to worry—what if my brother overhears someone talking about me? I didn't want him to hear that from someone other than me. So I told him.

"He started to cry, and I couldn't stand it. I got up and went on a walk by myself. After a while I walked to another friend's house, and the word had spread. The one friend I'd told had told other people, and it seemed like everyone knew. They were all crying. That was awful, too. Mostly it was weird because they'd all been drinking, and they were way too emotional, you know? It wasn't helping at all.

"I mean, by that time, I was better—I wasn't as upset as I had been. I'm not sure why—I think it was because even though the doctor had told me I was going to die, I didn't believe it, not deep down. I didn't feel sick. And I didn't feel any different than before he told me that news. So I guess it hadn't sunk in—it was just—I don't know, just unreal.

"Anyway, my friends and I gradually got it down to a normal level, where we weren't being sad and focusing on it, you know? They all said they weren't going to let me die and that they really believed I could get better. I guess I believe that, too."

A NEW CHANCE

Evidently so do some of her doctors at this new hospital. Kristin says that she got a late start here because—ironically—she wasn't sick enough at first.

"It took awhile for the doctors to let me get started here," she says. "These doctors took more scans, to see where we were, and you know what? There was no active tumor. Here I was, all happy to be doing something positive, to start getting better, and the tumor wasn't even there! They said I couldn't start treatment here until my tumor was active again. My mom laughed and said that the special herbal tea—essiac, it's called—that was what made the tumor go inactive. Whatever it was—what bad timing!

"So two weeks later, or somewhere around there, we had more scans that told us it had grown a little. We didn't come all the way out here for the scans—we just went back to that hospital in Philadelphia. Anyway, those new scans showed that the tumor was active—normally bad news, but now it was kind of a relief!"

Kristin interrupts herself. "Oh, I forgot something," she says. "When we were back for the day in Philadelphia, I ran into that one doctor when I was having my scans—you know, the one who told me the bad news? Anyway, he asked me what my reasoning was—why I decided to go all the way out here from the East Coast. He said, 'Do you really want to disrupt your family like this?'

"That made me so mad!" fumes Kristin. "I told him, 'I'm not disrupting my family—the cancer is!' I mean, I'm fighting it—does he think I should just roll over and give up? I think that doctor just didn't like the idea that we were going somewhere else. Maybe it makes him look bad. I know they asked us at one point what kind of chemo I was going to get at the new hospital. When we told them, they said, 'Oh, we can do that here, you know.' But my family was like, 'Yeah, but you told her she was going to die, so we're done with you.'"

THIRTY PERCENT

Kristin rubs her forehead, clearly agitated. "I really hated dealing with those guys. I'm so glad I don't have to anymore. My doctors here are nice. And the chemo I'm on isn't really new—it's just one that's being used in a new way.

"See, this is the chemo they usually just give to patients with lung cancer. I guess they've found that it works for people with Hodgkin's, too. So they're having some luck with it. People are getting better—at least some of them are—and I'm hoping that one of them will be me.

"I don't just have one doctor—there's a bunch. They're all nice, really. The doctor that designed this cancer center, the main guy, is one of my doctors. He's cautious, that's the only thing. Like, he admitted me to the hospital because he thought I had pneumonia.

Kristin worries that living at the Ronald McDonald House is boring for her brother but believes "he's better off here than just being home, wondering what's happening."

But I didn't. He said he just wanted to be safe. I understand that— and even though I didn't want to go into the hospital that time, I completely understood why he was being careful.

"And these doctors are pretty confident. They are honest, and they tell you all the time what's going on and what to expect— things like that. So that's what I'm doing now, just going to treatments each day. Not on weekends, though. And I've got a 30 percent chance of surviving this. It may sound low to you, but to me, it's a lot better than zero. And it could go up, too, as they see my lab results later in January."

"KIDS COME, KIDS GO"

The routine is pretty simple, she says. She knows it is boring for her parents and her brother, and she feels bad about that. "We just couldn't imagine leaving him home all this time," Kristin explains. "It was hard for him to think about being on his own. So even though he runs out of stuff to do, I think he's better off here than just being home, wondering what's happening.

"During the day, he goes to classes—they provide that, which is good. When I'm not sleeping or going to treatment, I go downstairs to the workout room. I'm trying to get my knees stronger—the medicines I'm taking make my knee joints really sore. It's hard to walk. It got really bad for a while, and I had to use a wheelchair. But I'm going to get them stronger.

"Sometimes I play pool with my mom. Or I sit downstairs and talk to people. I've made friends, and when they're around, we hang out. My mom—what she does is clean. There's probably not a room in the hospital over there that's as clean as our room here—she's always dusting, polishing. There isn't much else for her to do, though. Same with my dad.

"There are really a lot of families here, but you don't see some of them. Maybe they just want to be private, or the kid is too sick to come out of the room much, I don't know. It's weird here, though, because even with the kids you get to be friends with, everything changes all the time. Kids come, kids go. Some have just left, gotten better and gone home. Others have died."

She reaches over to a framed picture on her nightstand.

"This kid here, the one with the face mask, that's Chad. He had leukemia—he was here the first time I was here. He seemed fine when he left. In fact, he and I left at the same time. I guess they'd run out of things to do for him, though. Later, when I came back to start treatment, I found out he'd passed away. I was pretty depressed about that—I figured he'd just keep going on, you know? It just seemed like he would."

"WHAT I ALWAYS WANTED TO DO"

Kristin says that being sick hasn't made her give up thinking about the future. She says there are a lot of things she's looking forward to. "One thing is that my sister's getting married," she says, grinning. "I just found out, in fact. His name is Mark, and he's a really nice guy. She's going to college right now, back in New Jersey. She was always going to study to be a social worker, but I think she's changed her mind—now she's going to be a teacher. Anyway, Mark once bought me a throw, you know, for the bed? It has Scooby Doo on it—he knows I love animals. He'll be a great brother-in-law.

"I'm looking forward to getting home, too; I have a dog named Salem back home and I really miss her. We got her because some guy threw her out of a truck on the road. I can't believe how mean people can be sometimes, you know? But Salem is great.

"And I've got a big black cat named Nicodemus—actually he's my sister Erin's. He's huge—forty pounds. And I have a guinea pig named Punxsutawney, after the groundhog, you know? So I'm a big animal lover. In fact, I always wanted to be a vet—that's what I hope to study someday. Maybe when I'm all grown up, I'll get a farm and I'll have a whole bunch of animals—as many as I want."

THINKING AHEAD

She runs her hand over her hair again.

"Another thing I am looking forward to is my hair growing in again," she admits. "And also, stopping this one medicine that makes me so hungry—plus making me retain so much water. I'm all puffy—I don't look like I really look.

"My pants don't fit, either—I can't get into my favorite jeans. I just end up wearing drawstring pants. But that will change when I'm off the medicine. And my energy will come back, I'm sure. Now I get so tired doing so little! The one thing I have the energy to do is watch television. And I've really become addicted to that.

"I've never watched TV like I watch it now," she says, laughing. "And I've discovered all these shows that I can't live without. I watch soaps a lot, like *Days of Our Lives* and my new favorite—*Passions*. That one's very, very weird. It has a witch in it, and a midget. He's a doll, I guess, named Timmy, and he walks around. I know it sounds strange, but it's really good. For some reason, you just never want to miss it."

WISHING

Christmas is five days away, and Kristin and her family will be here, at the Ronald McDonald House, she says. Chemotherapy cannot be interrupted, even for special holidays.

"I wish we could go home," she says. "But as you can see, we are doing the best we can for Christmas right here. We've got the tree, the lights and stuff going up the stairs to the loft. I think we're getting presents—the people here sent out a sheet of paper, asking what we wanted.

Kristin stands by the Christmas tree she and her family decorated in their apartment at the Ronald McDonald House.

"Back home, I'd just shop at the base or at the mall. It's nothing like the mall here—the Mall of America! I did get to go to Camp Snoopy, and that was a lot of fun. I love roller coasters, and they've got a good one. I have some little coupons for money off on rides, so maybe I'll have a chance to go back.

"You know, I was thinking the other day how if the cancer goes away and we leave here and go home, I can't think of anything big to do. That's funny, you know? Like a celebration or anything— nothing sounds that great. Mostly what I'd want to do is just go out and find my friends on the base, just walk to their houses and find them."

Does she ever call them from here? She shakes her head no.

"I don't call, no. Some of them work, and it's hard getting hold of them. I don't know—it's not the same talking on the phone. I just miss seeing them and being in a group of kids, you know. I love my family, but I really need that feeling of being in the middle of a group of friends.

"It's funny, because I used to think it was so boring living on a base. There wasn't much to do, other than what I told you, just hang at people's houses, watch movies, or whatever. A lot of kids drink or do drugs—I guess because they get bored. But me and my friends would go to the youth center and play basketball or pool or something.

"It wasn't so much that I miss particular activities." She shrugs. "I just miss being there and feeling like everyone I need is close. I was thinking that when we were at the mall the other day; I was looking at bunches of kids my age, and I thought they were pretty lucky. Not that they don't have cancer—I don't mean that. Just that they're laughing and having fun, just being teenagers, like they're supposed to."

Cullen

"AS LONG AS THE CANCER
DOESN'T COME BACK, I'LL NEVER
HAVE CHEMO AGAIN. THAT'S SUCH
A GOOD FEELING."

A college freshman who loves soccer, Cullen was diagnosed with leukemia when he was just beginning high school. He has done well with his treatments, and is optimistic about his future. Now, he admits, he's frustrated by fatigue that still holds him back on the playing field.

"Cullen? Yeah, he's upstairs here," says the boy with the red hat pointing to a doorway behind him. "Just go up those stairs there, up to the fifth floor. Just yell when you get up there, and someone will tell you which room."

The college dorm is fairly quiet, for this is finals week. Most residents are either in their rooms with doors closed or off in a corner of the library. Cullen materializes in the doorway of the first room on the fifth floor and invites me in.

"Watch out for the couch," he says, offering a chair. "It's pretty saggy. Pretty questionable springs, I guess. But I like the room—I've got the whole thing to myself. I had a roommate at first, but he was doing some stuff that looked like he was going to get in trouble for. Or *we* might get in trouble for, if I'd stayed there. So I talked to someone, kind of a resident adviser, you know? He said, 'Good decision,' and he gave me the OK to move in here."

Cullen is an eighteen-year-old freshman with an athlete's build and an engaging grin. A member of the college soccer team, he has also spent the past few years battling cancer and doesn't mind talking about it.

"FOR ME IT WAS APRIL 4, 1997"

"It was a pretty major part of my life for the past few years," he says. "The kind I had was leukemia—acute lymphocytic leukemia. I guess pretty much everybody who has a life-threatening disease

Eighteen-year-old Cullen was diagnosed with acute lymphocytic leukemia at age fourteen.

or has a major injury or something—they could all tell you the exact date of when it happened, or when they found out what it was. For me it was April 4, 1997. I was almost fifteen—it was almost the end of my first year of high school.

"One of the things about this kind of cancer, I guess, is that it's pretty hard to diagnose. I mean, there are symptoms that kind of coincide with other diseases, so it doesn't seem obvious to anybody that you're really seriously sick. And that's the part that made it such a nightmare for my family—I'd had leukemia since the past Thanksgiving. That's a pretty long time to be sick and not be diagnosed."

A PERSISTENT VIRUS?

Cullen says it started when he had what seemed like the flu at Thanksgiving. "I had a really upset stomach and was throwing up all weekend," he says. "I felt better after a few days, so it just seemed like it was a virus. But I never really felt 100 percent better, you know? It just seemed to hang on—being tired and stuff.

"My family—that's my mom and dad and my sister, Krystal, and me—we all went out to California for Christmas. That's where my mom's family lives. And I just felt—I don't know—just sort of lousy. Every day it seemed like I was tired and kind of dragging through the day. So when we came back home, my mom made an appointment to take me in to the doctor.

"Anyway, they were pretty reassuring. They just said it was a virus, kind of a persistent one, I guess. But the weeks were going by, and I wasn't feeling any better. By the middle of January, I was all yellowish—that's a sign of being jaundiced. Your liver produces too much of something."

He thinks for a moment. "I think it's bilirubin. Yeah, I'm pretty sure that's it. Anyway, your liver is out of whack or something, and you get too much of that stuff and your skin looks yellow. My friends at school were all kidding me about it, I remember."

"I WAS MISSING A LOT OF STUFF"

Cullen remembers that the doctors assumed that whatever virus he had before was now in his liver. "So we started seeing liver specialists," he says. "They told us that it was mono, but my mom wasn't buying it. See, I wasn't sleeping all the time, and that's what you think of with mono. I mean, you can't get enough sleep, supposedly. But that wasn't me. I wasn't sleepy—I was just tired out. No ambition.

"I wasn't missing school or anything. But after school, I'd come home and just sort of flop on the couch and do nothing. I didn't have the energy. But I wasn't sleeping. And I sure wasn't putting out much energy—I'd be up watching television or whatever till two or three in the morning on weekends. So mono didn't seem right.

"But the tests that they did showed mono, and so we went home and figured that I'd get better after the mono went away. But it kept up and kept up. It was really a drag, too, because I was missing a lot of stuff that I really enjoyed. I still hung out with all my friends, but other than renting movies or just sitting around, there was nothing I felt like doing."

No Soccer

Soccer has always been his passion, and Cullen says he missed out on a lot of soccer that winter. "I was playing soccer year-round, you know—outside in nice weather, and in the winter I was on a team that played indoors. Plus, I'd made this special team called ODP—that's short for Olympic Development Program. Guys all over the state try out just to get in ODP; I'd made it, but on weekends when they practiced, I was too tired to do anything. I tried, because I really wanted to be there, but I couldn't do much.

"I was getting really discouraged because of that. I'd always dreamed of playing Division I soccer, you know, at the most competitive level. And being in ODP is supposed to really help you get to that ability, if you're willing to work hard. But it was pretty clear that I couldn't keep up. So I dropped out of ODP, dropped off my winter team."

Doctors and More Doctors

All the while, Cullen's parents were making appointments to see other doctors—anyone who could explain why a case of the flu in November had evolved into jaundice, mono, and a new variation—bone pain.

"That was horrible," he says, remembering. "My legs just hurt so much—especially back when I'd been trying to play a little soccer. I'd run a little, and then I'd have to stop. And then that night, I'd wake up like at two in the morning, crying. My knees and ankles were hurting so much, you wouldn't believe it. That couldn't be mono. But no one was really giving us answers to explain anything.

"I mean, the doctors would say, 'Oh, he probably pulled a muscle.' They didn't get it at all. And back when they were figuring out about my liver, one of the doctors even suggested my problem was

A persistent virus, extreme fatigue, and bone pain sent Cullen to several doctors who were initially unable to explain his symptoms.

related to drug use. Like I was taking drugs or something. It was ridiculous. They didn't know anything.

"Anyway, my mom and dad wouldn't let it ride—they'd try to get to the bottom of it. They knew it wasn't drugs, it wasn't pulled muscles. This going-to-the-doctor thing was getting to be a major activity. I was missing a lot of school—not from being sick, but from the doctor appointments.

Every week we'd go in to the hematologist, so they could do blood work to check my liver. Mostly my mom would go with me—my dad is a dentist, and it's hard for him to be out of the office as often as I needed to go to the doctor! Anyway, the blood counts showed that the infection or whatever in my liver was kind of up and down, I guess. Sometimes I'd seem better (as far as the numbers went) and other times I seemed worse."

Cullen tilts back in his chair, balancing on the back legs. "But in March I got *really* sick. And then things started happening fast."

"Your Son Is Gravely Ill"

The event that seemed to start everything in motion, says Cullen, was getting fitted for contact lenses. "I was looking forward to it—I'd be able to see without wearing glasses when I played soccer," he says. "But what happened was right after I got fitted for the contacts, I got a major eye infection. Not just red, but swollen and really disgusting. The antibiotics we got didn't help at all, and my mom had had it by then.

"We went back to the doctor and she said, 'Look, nothing is working. He's worse, not better. Nothing you are doing is working at all.' The doctor said, 'Let's let the hematologist do his last test—that's coming up next week.' My mom said fine, he could do the test—but not next week. 'Now,' is what she said. She told him my eye was infected, and my sinuses were really, really infected. I was sick, and they needed to figure it out.

"So we did that blood test two days later, on a Friday. My mom and dad both came with me—we got in, the doctor took a blood smear, and then while he was off testing it, we were just sitting in his office, my parents and me. Anyway, about a half hour later, the doctor comes in and says to them, 'Your son is gravely ill.' And I thought, 'What? What's the matter with me?'"

Never Thought of Cancer

The doctor informed them that Cullen was most likely suffering from either leukemia or aplastic anemia. What surprised Cullen was that the doctor was hoping for leukemia.

"I knew leukemia was a kind of cancer," he says, "and I couldn't believe anything was as bad as cancer. But evidently this aplastic anemia was a lot harder to treat—it has to do with your body not producing enough red blood cells. So anyway, what the doctor was going to do was a bone marrow biopsy. By looking at a piece of my bone marrow, he'd be able to tell what the problem really was.

"So they took me on a gurney from the doctor's office to the hospital, since they were connected. I don't remember much after that; I was sedated for the biopsy, and later I'm in this hospital room and my mom is there. The doctor comes in and says I have leukemia—and he's relieved. I remember my mom being really stunned. She told me later that she never ever suspected cancer—even with all the uncertainty and everything. Cancer was never one of the options in her mind.

"So she was stunned, and I was groggy. I really didn't get what was going on. And after the doctor talks and talks, she says, 'So you are saying Cullen has cancer?' And he's like, 'Yeah.' And then she was crying, and I was crying, too. I remember being in that room, and it was getting dark outside, and we didn't know what to do. That was one of the worst times, I think."

"WHAT WOULD YOU DO?"

Cullen says that feeling of helplessness didn't last long. His mother went out to the nurses' station after he fell asleep and talked to one of the nurses on duty. "She asked her if she had kids, and the nurse said she did," says Cullen. "And my mom asked her what she would do if it happened to one of her kids. The nurse didn't even hesitate. She just said, 'I'd get him right over to the Children's Hospital—they're great over there.' See, at the hospital where I was, there were hardly any kids. But at Children's, that's all they did.

"So that's what happened. I went over there and got going with Dr. Joann Hilden—she was my new doctor. It was a relief to have someone that really knew what was going on, after so many months of confusion. She said that the very next day I was going to start chemotherapy, and they'd start getting me healthy again.

"Dr. Hilden said that what I was going to have was a three-year protocol. That didn't mean that I'd be in the hospital for three years, but that I'd be having treatment and care for the cancer for that length of time. Jeez, that seemed like a long time, when she said that. I remember thinking, 'I'll be eighteen by the time I'm done with this stuff!'"

"PEOPLE DON'T KNOW WHAT TO THINK"

He was also thinking about his friends from school. How would they find out this news? Should he just call them and tell them what was going on?

"I'd always been really close to my friends," he says. "And even though they knew I'd been going to doctors for the past several months trying to figure out why I was so tired and everything, I was sure they would be floored by hearing I had cancer. People don't know what to think, you know?

"As it turned out, my parents called my friends. I found that out the next day, when a whole bunch of them came to the hospital. I mean, there's like eight guys that show up in my room all of a sudden, and I figured out what was going on. It was maybe awkward in there for a few minutes, but it didn't take long for us to be talking and laughing—although I was pretty tired.

After being diagnosed with cancer, Cullen began a three-year treatment program that included chemotherapy.

"The other thing that happened with my friends had to do with the hospital staff. There is this program or service, I guess you'd call it, where a lady goes to your school and talks to kids about what's going on. She came to me first and asked for permission—I don't know, maybe some kids wouldn't have wanted something like that. But it was a no-brainer for me—I thought it was a great idea.

"So what happened was they made an announcement that during fourth period, anyone could go down to this one classroom and ask questions. So all my friends, all the kids who knew me or were interested at all—they went down. The lady told them that a classmate of theirs, Cullen, has leukemia. And she told them what it was, what the prognosis was, what I'd be doing at the hospital, stuff like that. They had an hour and a half to ask whatever questions they wanted to.

"My friends told me afterward that it was great. Since I wasn't there, kids could ask questions without—I don't know—without worrying about making me feel weird. Like was I going to die, or what would happen to my hair, and questions like that. Anyway, a lot of people showed up, even a couple of teachers. So it felt more comfortable for me, knowing that people knew about me."

STARTING CHEMO

While his friends were hearing about his illness, Cullen was beginning the treatments intended to kill the cancer cells. He says he had heard of chemotherapy but wasn't too nervous about starting it.

"I don't think I felt well enough to worry," he admits. "I'm not by nature a real pessimistic person anyway—maybe that's part of it. But the doctors and everyone were real positive. So I just took my cues from the people around me. They told me what to expect—the hair might fall out, the feeling sick, the being tired. Actually, I didn't think it was too bad at first. I was OK for about a week, and then all of a sudden, I felt just like they said I would.

"The doctors also talked to me about the importance of moving around. They said that the more I get up and walk around during this part of the treatment, the less muscle loss and everything that I'd have later on. For someone like me, who wanted to play competitive sports, that was really important, because it meant that I could get back into soccer more quickly."

Cullen smiles, rolling his eyes. "So I'm like, 'OK, I'm going to do eight laps around the hospital every day.' I really thought

Chemotherapy drained Cullen of his energy. Now finished with his treatment, he is still struggling to regain his strength.

that was going to happen. But then after the chemo started, I tried walking around once, and I thought, 'I'm not going anywhere—I feel lousy.' So I kind of did the lap between my hospital bed and the bathroom to throw up. That was my exercise program."

EXTRA MEDICINE

Although he was given antinausea medication along with his chemotherapy, Cullen found it ineffective.

"Yeah," he says with a grin. "That's a good word for it—that's putting it mildly! The weird thing about that stuff was that the first six months I did chemo, I took antinausea stuff. And even when they gave me a month off—they do that occasionally to let your body recover—I was puking all the time. And the doctors couldn't understand why at first, but then they figured it out—I was getting sick *because* of the antinausea medicine. I was better off without it. Too bad it took six months to get that straight. Anyway, the doctors found a combination of three different things that seemed to work.

"I took steroids, too. That's another common thing with people on chemo. See, the chemo kills every fast-reproducing cell in your body. The target is cancer cells, of course, but it also gets hair cells in there, as well as fingernail cells. That's why hair falls out. And my fingernails didn't grow at all the whole time I was doing chemo. But the chemo also kills white blood cells. And they're a lot more important than hair cells and fingernail cells, because they fight infection.

"So your body just naturally fights the chemo, because it thinks the chemo is an invader. Which I guess it is. Anyway, the chemo

During his hospitalization, Cullen's mother spent as much time with him as she could, often sleeping on the couch in his room.

can't do its thing with the body fighting it. So they give you steroids like prednisone or whatever—that stuff kills the part of your body that fights off the chemo."

Beefy Nachos and Other Cravings

He explains that although the steroids are helpful, they also produce various side effects. "The big puffy cheeks, that's one," he says. "That's because the medicine makes your body retain water. And you kind of get this watermelon belly, too. And the steroids really make you hungry—just so hungry you can't imagine it. I'd eat enormous amounts of food, and then I'd go throw up—that was from the chemo. And anyway, I'm in the middle of throwing up, and all I can think of is how good some beefy nachos would taste.

"So I'm calling downstairs, 'Mom, would you make me some nachos?' It was bizarre. It's like cravings, like you hear about pregnant women. This one day I'd had a dream about those beefy nachos—I'd had them in the school cafeteria once. And this was before nine in the morning that I needed those nachos. My mom was calling all over town, looking for anyplace that would turn on their ovens and make me beefy nachos.

"There are stories about people who have had to put a padlock on their refrigerators," he says, warming to the topic. "I mean, a kid on steroids will come down in the middle of the night and eat their whole fridge. It's amazing how much food you can put away, too. I heard about one kid in chemo who ate three twelve-inch subs in one sitting—before he threw up."

Cullen grins. "And then he probably wanted three more."

Hospital Time

After a month on chemotherapy, his bone marrow was checked again to see if any cancer cells remained. The news, says Cullen, was good. "No, I didn't have any cells left," he says. "If the chemo works that fast on you, they call you a rapid reactor, I think. Anyway, that meant that I could go home and start the chemo on an outpatient schedule. I was glad to be leaving—it seemed like I'd been there forever at that point.

"To my parents—especially my mom—I'm sure it seemed like even longer than that. My mom doesn't work outside our home, so she was able to spend a lot more time there than my dad. But he usually came over at lunchtime and then went back to work. My mom slept at the hospital every night I was there—on a lumpier couch than that one," he says, pointing to the sofa next to the wall.

"I remember someone telling me that when that lady from the hospital came to my school, one of the kids asked why I had to be in the hospital so long if I was just taking medicine. It seems strange, maybe—except there are so many things the doctors have to be concerned about. Like if you get a cold or something—anything can be dangerous when you don't have enough white blood cells to help your immune system.

"And you can get dehydrated really easily, too. Even throwing up, you lose water, and that's no good when you're sick. So they check that stuff, check your blood all the time to see if your counts are low enough to mean you need a transfusion or something. I guess they can do that easier at a hospital; easier than having a doctor following you around all day.

"Plus, for me there was this extra thing," Cullen says. "You know how on television, when they're advertising some medicine and they warn about how a small percentage of people may experience side effects? Well, that's me. I'm that 'small percentage of people.' No matter what medicine I get, I'll get the weird side effect. One drug turned me into a diabetic temporarily—I even had to take insulin. Others gave me bad rashes and headaches. You name it, I always got it. So I was kind of a challenge to the doctors, I guess."

THE HAIR

His hair fell out, he says, although not right away. Cullen says that he had a system for keeping his hair—a system that appeared to be working, at least at first. "I figured out that it wouldn't fall out if you didn't touch it," he says. "During the first round of chemo, this was. Anyway, mine just sort of stayed up there, just—I don't know—just hanging on, I guess. But if I touched my head at all, like scratched my head or anything, it would come out.

"But my system kind of crashed during the second round of chemo," he admits ruefully. "I lost all my hair then. It was coming out in the shower, on the pillow, wherever. And eventually someone came to my room and just shaved it off, since it looked so strange by then."

Did his baldness bother him? Cullen admits that at first it made him feel strange. "I remember the first time I went out bald," he

While undergoing chemotherapy, Cullen had the same worries as many other cancer patients, such as how people would react to seeing him bald.

says. "Some friend of my parents had invited us out to some country club for dinner. It was the first time I'd been out socially since I'd lost my hair, where no one knew me. I remember thinking, 'Should I wear a hat?' Because you see that, you know, sometimes. But then I thought that it would seem strange to be wearing a hat at the country club, eating dinner.

"So I just said, 'OK, I'm going bald.' And I just got dressed up and went like I was. People looked at me; I just looked back at them. In my mind I was telling them, 'Yeah, I'm bald. So what?' Maybe some people thought I'd shaved it, but I'm sure most figured out I had cancer."

"I NEVER KNOW HOW I'LL FEEL ABOUT IT"

Cullen says that he had some of the same worries before going back to school the following year. He'd missed the rest of his freshman year after being diagnosed, and he went back on a part-time basis his sophomore year.

"I'd come to school a couple of times for visits, before I started back as a student," he says. "I already knew that my friends would be OK—I mean, I looked different, but they knew I was the same guy I was before. When my mom drove up to the school, a bunch of the kids came outside. They looked at me kind of strange—I could tell they were like, 'Wow, those are some big cheeks on that bald kid!' They knew what to expect, but I think knowing and seeing are different. I understood their shock—I'd look in the mirror and I'd be thinking the same thing.

"But it didn't take long for that stuff to go away. The harder part is looking different around the people you don't know, like I said. I never know how I'll feel about it. Some days I'd put a stocking cap on and go to the mall, just get whatever I had to and then get out of there, you know? I'd be thinking that I didn't want to see the looks some of those people had in their eyes.

"But other times I want people to see me. It's like I want to say, 'Yeah, some people *do* have cancer and they do normal stuff like this, like go to the mall. Like me—and are you going to look at me weird now?' It's like I sort of felt proud. It's hard to explain."

A DREAM COME TRUE

What about soccer? How long did it take for him to feel well enough to play?

"That first summer after I was diagnosed, I didn't play at all, and that was really rough," he says. "I'd been playing summer soccer since I was a little kid, and it seemed so weird not to be going to practices or thinking about tournaments. But I went to most of the games to cheer my team on. I'd pull out my little chair and sit and watch. I felt pretty crappy, but it was so nice to just think about playing again.

"One really amazing thing happened that summer, too. There's this tournament called the U.S.A. Cup—it's the largest youth soccer tournament in the world, I think. Kids from every country you can think of come here to play. And my team had always participated. Usually they try to get some famous player or coach to come to the opening ceremonies—a torch thing kind of like the Olympics—and that summer Pelé was going to be there. Pelé! He's the best there ever was, you know?

"Anyway, the coach of my summer team was part of the organizing committee for this tournament, and he got it arranged where I'd be the one to bring the torch into the stadium. He told them that I was a huge soccer enthusiast and couldn't play this year. So they let me do that—I brought the torch up to the podium where Pelé was standing.

"I was really supposed to just bring the torch, but when I handed it to him, he said, 'Come on up here.' I said, 'What?' And he motioned for me to come back. So I thought, 'All right.' It was so strange, looking around that packed stadium and seeing all those people cheering. I got a letter from him later and an autographed ball. People talk about 'a dream come true'—that really was, for me."

Changes Because of Cancer

Asked if he is a different person because of his experience with cancer, Cullen doesn't hesitate. "There have been, yeah"—he nods—"some small things, others not so small. One thing that was hard was being so close to my family when I was really sick and sort of withdrawing from my friends. It wasn't like I wanted to withdraw—it just happened naturally. I mean, I wasn't doing much of anything they were—in school or out.

"My mom and I really got tight. She was always there for me, like I said. She took a lot of crap from me, when I was cranky and feeling lousy. But then, once I started feeling better and was doing a less-intense chemotherapy, I got back tighter with my friends again. That was hard for her. I'm sure she felt like she'd been dumped for all these friends of mine. I know she was hurt, even though she understood.

"I learned that I really needed to figure things out for myself, too. There were people on the staff of that hospital who offered to help with aspects of my going back to school, or playing on the soccer team, or whatever. There were counselors, people like that. But I never really used them. I wasn't depressed—at least, not often. I liked to work things out myself. I don't think I bottle things up inside—it's more like listening to your own inner voices, I think."

STRENGTH FROM DIFFERENT SOURCES

Asked if he considered himself religious, Cullen nods. "Yeah, I guess I'm fairly religious," he says guardedly. "I don't go to church. I used to, but back then I wasn't really religious. But I pray every day. I never prayed back in the days when I went to church.

"You know, when I was sick, people would send me these cards, like the ones of the saints, you know? And I got four cards of Saint Peregrine; he's the saint you pray to if you have cancer, I guess. There's a little prayer on the back of the cards to say about helping you deal with things, how to get better. I just put it by my bed and kept it there. I felt like it helped. I don't know—it's hard to say. But I looked at it all the time.

"Maybe that helped me. But also, I think a sense of humor really helps, too. I've always been sort of a comedian. Maybe 'smart-ass'

Cullen and his grandmother shop for healthful food to include in his diet during his recovery.

is the term I'm looking for. I think there's strength in that, too. Wherever the strength comes from, I'm cancer-free now. I'm done with chemo—it took more than three years, but I'm done. As long as the cancer doesn't come back, I'll never have chemo again. That's such a good feeling—you have no idea."

"Get the Book and Read Chapter 6"

Even though he is healthy today, Cullen admits there are parts of his life that are still not the same. "I still have to go in to the doctor more often than other people," he says. "I go in once a month for blood work; they check my lymph nodes and have me breathe in the nebulizer. The nebulizer prevents pneumonia. People usually do that by pill, but I get sick from the pill—I told you I get weird reactions!

"Because my blood counts are lower than most people's, I still have to be really careful about not getting sick. That makes my mom nuts, worrying about that—especially because I'm not home where she can keep an eye on all that stuff like she used to."

Cullen looks serious for a moment. "There have been times when I feel amazingly distant from other people. It's like no one knew exactly how it felt when I was going through it. And at the same time, it was really hard to talk about—even with my family.

"Anyway, not long ago, I read a biography of Lance Armstrong—he's the bicycle racer who had cancer. The book's called *It's Not About the Bike: My Journey Back to Life*. Anyway, when I read chapter 6—it's called 'Chemo'—I thought, 'What he's saying is exactly right.' See, when he visualized everything that was happening to him, that's what I was thinking, too.

"I don't want to always be talking about cancer with them, about did I take my pills or how do I feel. If I keep talking about it, it's like I'm experiencing it all over again. And I don't want that at all. So Lance Armstrong said this so well—I wanted my parents to read this. So I told them, 'Get the book and read chapter 6.' So they did, I guess—they bought it, and on the way home from the store, my mom was reading it out loud to my dad. And they had to pull over to the side, because I guess it hit them pretty hard, what he wrote."

The Grand Scheme

He sits for a moment, lost in a thought. And then he grins. "I'm also a lot more laid-back than I ever was before," he says. "The little things in life don't worry me. Like a test doesn't stress me out

Now a college freshman, Cullen has been studying science but his interests have recently turned to mathematics.

like it does other guys. Now, for instance, we're in finals week, and lots of the guys on my floor are nuts. They're panicking, losing sleep, worrying about what will happen.

"But not me. I don't mean that I don't care—I do. I just don't want to worry about something like a test. In the grand scheme of things, it just isn't that big a deal. And when I drive somewhere with my mom and she gets a red light or something, she kind of hits the steering wheel and cusses, and I'm like, 'Mom, you're going to get an ulcer—just lay back and chill.'

"There's a lot of good stuff going on—I'm here at college, doing fine. Well—fine, relatively speaking. Up until last Tuesday, I could have even told you what I was majoring in—science. I've always wanted to be a dentist, like my dad."

He grins again. "A lot of my parents' friends are dentists, and it seems like the perfect job. I mean, sitting in your little back room playing on the computer all day, and then come out and say a couple of words to the patient. And then go back to the computer. What a cake job!

"But then last Tuesday, I'm sitting in this chemistry/physics lecture. And it dawns on me that it had taken me a full minute to understand the last sentence the professor said. And I thought, 'Hey, I don't really *like* science!' So dentistry is out. Maybe I'll do something with numbers—I'm good in math. So I'll come up with a new plan."

"I'M NOT 100 PERCENT YET"

"But soccer is definitely in my future. I played on the college team this fall. I'm not 100 percent yet—in fact, when I came at the end of the summer to try out, I flunked all the speed trials, all that endurance stuff. Slowest kid on the team, can't do the two-mile run, on and on. And that's discouraging, because that's not really me. Or at least, that's not who I was. I can't play a full soccer game yet—I don't have the energy.

"But I will. The coach has kind of taken me on like a project, I think. He's setting me up with a speed coach in the off-season, so I can make a comeback by next fall. And in the meantime, I'm really enjoying college. I feel good; I've got a lot of friends. I've got a lot of things to be happy about."

Daniel

"I'D NEVER REALLY THOUGHT
ABOUT BEING A DOCTOR BEFORE,
BUT NOW I'M PRETTY SURE IT'S
WHAT I WANT TO BE."

At fifteen, Daniel is in the final stage of his chemotherapy. He was diagnosed with leukemia in sixth grade and says his family and friends were key factors in keeping his spirits up through the long treatments.

Daniel has been trying to explain how he was diagnosed with cancer—only the phone keeps ringing. "Sorry," he says, and dashes to answer it. It's another friend, wanting to know what movie they're going to see, and whether Daniel can sleep over afterward. He makes his plans quickly and slips back into the chair across from me.

"That was Bobby," he explains. "I've been trying to get ahold of him for the last hour, so I had to talk. There's probably going to be a bunch more guys calling, but I'll just call them back later."

A diminished social life doesn't seem to be an effect of having cancer as a teenager, right? Daniel grins.

"No," he says. "I guess not."

"I'M STILL BATTLING CANCER"

Daniel is a good-looking boy, with sandy brown hair and a smile that goes right into his eyes. He has no trouble maintaining a conversation with an unusually nosy adult—he says he figures it might be good for him to talk about his illness.

"I'm still battling cancer," he says. "It's cancer of the blood—leukemia. I'm still taking chemo for it; I take two-and-a-half pills every night. And once a month I go into the hospital to get a shot of another medicine in my spine. See, the spine is where cancer cells can hide—even if they've been knocked out of every other place in your body, they might be there. So I get a spinal tap every three months, just to check.

"The shot goes in here," he says, pointing to a spot near his hip bone, "just about an inch above where your hip bone kind of joins your leg. And the spinal tap—it would probably hurt a lot, only they give you something to relax. It's not my favorite thing to go

Daniel is still struggling with cancer and receives chemotherapy and daily medication.

through, but it's not terrible. Compared to other stuff I've had to do, it isn't the worst, believe me!"

A BAD COLD

Daniel learned that he had cancer when he was in sixth grade, just a few days after his twelfth birthday. But later he learned that he'd had cancer for some time before doctors realized what it was.

"I'd been sick with a bad cold," he says. "A cough and everything. My mom took me to the doctor because of the cough, because a couple of kids at my school had had walking pneumonia, so she wanted to see if there was medicine I should be taking. But it wasn't anything—at least that's what the pediatrician said. Just a bad cold.

"And then a couple of days later, some lymph nodes were swollen—you know the ones on the sides of your neck? They swell up when your body is fighting an infection. Well, those were enlarged, and so were the lymph glands in the back of my neck. So my mom called about that, too—but they figured it was because of the cold and because I also have allergies. I think they told my mom that if they didn't go away in a few days, she should bring me in."

"IT FELT LIKE A BRUISE"

Sandy, Daniel's mother, has been working in another part of the house; she hears what he's saying and acknowledges that they felt reassured by the doctor's advice.

"It's funny how when a doctor or a nurse tells you something, you really relax. I felt like, 'OK, they're telling me this is not unusual to have these symptoms.' But later, like Dan said, we found out that when he'd been sick with that cold, he'd had full-blown leukemia. I don't mean that the cold was leukemia. But the cold was much more severe *because* of the leukemia."

Dan says that a few days afterward, he was sitting in class and he felt a sore, swollen area on his neck.

"It felt like a bruise, I guess," he says. "I was scratching my neck or something, and I felt it. It was really sore right where those glands are. But it was a lump—a pretty big one, too. It kind of made me wonder, because it really appeared fast—I hadn't felt it when I woke up or anything. Anyway, I told my teacher about it, and she let me go down to the nurse.

"The nurse looked at it, but since I wasn't feeling sick or anything, she said I could go back to class. She told me to have my parents check with the doctor later on. So that's what I did. I didn't really think that much about it after that—I just went through the rest of the day."

"I WASN'T WORRIED"

Daniel's dad took him to the doctor after school. A nurse drew blood, he says, and she was gone for a little while after that.

"When the doctor came back in, he was pretty serious," Daniel remembers. "He said that he didn't know for sure what I had—it could be lots of things—but he wanted me to get checked out by a specialist. He said it was maybe nothing serious at all, but when my dad was asking questions, the doctor did say leukemia was a possibility."

Didn't that frighten him, to hear that it could be leukemia? Daniel shakes his head.

"I wasn't worried," he says. "I mean, I didn't feel bad. I didn't really know what it was—I knew it was a kind of cancer and everything, but I didn't know how serious it was. Maybe if I'd known all I know now, I'd have been scared. But see, the doctor wasn't saying he thought it was leukemia. It was just one of a bunch of possibilities.

"After a while my dad talked to the doctor while I went out to the waiting room. He told me afterward that he wanted to see if the doctor was thinking anything he didn't want to say before, while I was there, you know? But I guess there wasn't anything else. So we went home."

"YOU HEAR ABOUT CANCER . . . AND EVERYBODY JUST FALLS APART"

Later that evening he and his parents talked a little about going to Children's Hospital the next day. His mother and father talked to him about some of the things the doctor had said.

"They asked me if I remembered what leukemia was," says Dan. "Because we'd known two people who had it—a substitute teacher at school, her son had it. And some friends of our family—they have a son who has it, too. And my mom told me about the kind of ways they treat people with cancer, and stuff like that. They weren't trying to scare me—I think they were just letting me know what the possibilities were.

Because he didn't feel sick at the time, Daniel says he wasn't scared when he was diagnosed with cancer.

"Well, the next morning we went to the hospital, and I found out pretty quick that it was leukemia, all right. I'd had another bunch of blood taken, and this doctor named Dr. Anne Bendel came out and talked to us. It's so funny—that part wasn't scary at all, not like you'd think it would be.

"I mean, you hear about cancer, and it's a different thing, like a death sentence, and everybody just falls apart. But that's not how Dr. Bendel was at all. She was just—I don't know—she was really eager to get down to business. And her business was getting me fixed up, to get rid of the cancer. She said we'd caught it early, and it was very treatable. So how can you get scared over that?"

He takes a long sip from a glass of water. "She's a little shorter than me, Dr. Bendel. She's still my doctor, and I'm really glad. I liked her right off the bat, and so did my parents. She's kind; I guess that's the main thing. And she's like a mom—I mean, she *is* a mom, but she acts like she cares as much about me as one of her own kids.

"Anyway, instead of being sad and scared and falling apart, I was sort of excited to be doing something new. I don't mean really happy-excited; I just felt like it was all strange and I was interested in what was going to happen. I met the nurses who would be taking care of me, and I got checked into the hospital right then! I guess, looking back, if I hadn't had my parents there or if I hadn't had a nice doctor, I'd have been scared. But it was OK."

THE PLAN

Daniel says that he learned right away that what he had was called acute lymphoblastic leukemia, or ALL, for short. It is one of the most common types of cancer among children and teenagers.

"While we were going up to the eighth floor—that's where the cancer patients were—the doctor told me what the plan was. I was going to be there at the hospital a pretty long time at first—from two weeks to a month, maybe.

"That was surprising to me, I guess. I was thinking, 'What can they possibly do to me for a whole month? I'm not feeling sick or anything.' Well, at least I wasn't at first! I guess they took care of that pretty quickly, once I got started on the chemotherapy.

"But what they would do first, she said, was to take a sample of my bone marrow. That's a good place to see what percentage of cancer cells I had in there. That was just a long needle they'd stick into my hip, to take a little of the bone marrow out. They put me under to do that, so I didn't feel it at all.

"The news was that I had a pretty high percentage of cancer cells—92 percent. And even though that sounds really bad, I learned that it would go down really fast once they got me going on the medicine. And the plan was I'd stay on the medicine until all those cancer cells were gone. If any were still there, like in my spine—remember?—they could come back later and make me sick all over again. So they had to get every one."

SICK AND TIRED—AND A QUESTION

What made the chemotherapy powerful against cancer cells made it even stronger against the healthy cells in his body, says Daniel.

"I went from feeling not that bad to feeling pretty awful," he admits. "They put a thing in my chest—I still have it here. In fact, I get it out next month—that will be nice! It's really just tubes that IVs can go in, so they don't have to stick me with a needle every time. Then they hooked me up to the chemo medicine. And also, I was getting a lot of fluids to keep me hydrated. It's not healthy for anybody to not have enough water in them, but especially when you're on chemo. You lose a lot of water, since you're always throwing up, or having diarrhea, or whatever. So getting extra fluid is important.

"So, when I wondered about what they'd do for me in the hospital, I found out pretty fast. Most of the time I didn't feel like doing much. I threw up about six times a day—but it was weird, because when I wasn't throwing up, I didn't feel sick. It wasn't like the flu, when you feel like when you're not throwing up that you have to. Lots of times, I was hungry in between, in fact.

"And all day the nurses and doctor would come in and check stuff. Sometimes it was blood pressure, or listening to my heart, or my lungs. Sometimes they'd draw blood and go check that. I mean, I wasn't busy, but they sure were."

Daniel says that the thing that worried him the most was losing his hair. He asked the nurses whether they thought he might keep his. "It was pretty much 'No,'" he says, smiling. "I was so disappointed, because that was so scary to me. I worried about looking different, looking weird. I'd get so worried sometimes that I'd have to force myself to stop thinking about it. But the answer was that I'd lose it, and it would grow back. It's funny, because lots of people think your hair falls out because of cancer. But it's the chemo that does it.

"But what I was going to say was it didn't fall out right away, right when I started the chemo. I think it was maybe two months after—and by then I was home. I remember thinking how glad I was that I'd gotten my school picture taken early in the fall, when I still had my hair—before all of this started."

A LOT OF SUPPORT

Daniel says that a lot of people made that time more bearable, just by being supportive. He was delighted by the visits, even though he wasn't feeling too well.

"Everyone was really great," he says. "My friends all came to visit, and my teacher from school. I had a lot of people who sent gifts and cards. A lot of my relatives came, and the ones who live far away called. It really helped cheer me up.

Daniel, here with his younger brother, says his family's support has made his treatment more bearable.

"My mom stayed every day at the hospital, and she slept there every night I was there. We'd watch all the daytime shows—I got hooked on some of them. I watched soap operas, which I can honestly say I don't watch anymore! Game shows were good, and some of the talk shows were amazing.

"There was this one channel on TV that was an in-house channel, and there'd be games for kids to play, like bingo and different things. That was cool. And like I said, I got presents. If I knew someone with a twelve-year-old boy with cancer, I'd suggest they buy some handheld games—those were fun. And some of those drawing things—magic ink, or whatever. I don't play with that kind of stuff much anymore, but they were really fun then."

Up and Around

Occasionally he would feel well enough to get out of bed, and he found some interesting things to do, he says. "There was a teen center on our floor," he says. "Technically, I wasn't allowed, because I wasn't thirteen yet, but there was a really nice guy who'd let me go in when there weren't a lot of people in there. The room had a Nintendo 64, air hockey, and a lot of comfortable chairs to just relax in.

"I met some other kids, too. They had cancer, too, but different kinds—some had tumors; some had bone cancer. I talked to them, because I'd think about something other than focusing on how I felt. That was my mom's idea. She thought it was important to connect like that—and I guess it was smart. Anyway, I met some nice kids in the teen center.

"And I also met some different doctors—that was because of Dr. Bendel. I mean, she was still my main doctor, but she was really good about introducing me to other doctors, just in case I'd need to be seen when she wasn't around. That was smart of her, I thought."

Not a Rapid Responder

One of the things the doctors were eager to learn was how quickly the chemo would affect Daniel's cancer. "They took a bone marrow scan right away, before the chemo—I told you about that," he says. "And then every once in a while, they'd do another scan to see what the count was. It dropped—it went from 92 to the fifties, then to the teens. And then to 8, and slowly down to zero.

"The way they figure out how long to do the chemo and everything is by looking at how fast the chemo works. There was one point, I think after day seven of the chemo, where they did a scan, and if I'd had under 25, I would have done one kind of treatment. But I wasn't that low—I was at 39. It took another two or three weeks for me to hit 25.

"So what that meant was that I wasn't what they call a 'rapid responder.' My risk was a little higher because of that, and so I'd have to have stronger chemo and do radiation therapy besides. The radiation is quite strong—it makes you sicker than the chemo did. But it didn't last that long, and I was really glad."

HOME, BUT TIRED

The plan has been for Daniel to have three years and two months of chemotherapy. The first year was the most intense.

"But at least after that first round, I got to go home," he says. "I'd go into the hospital as an outpatient for an hour or two for my chemo. Then home. I was so glad to be back home, but it's amazing how little energy I had.

Daniel is grateful that his mother stayed at the hospital during his chemotherapy. "She slept there every night I was there," he says.

"If I'd wanted to, I could have gone to school. But there was no way I could have. See, the chemo really lowers your energy. And your red blood count—that's what gives you your energy—that's supposed to be like 12 or 13 or something. Mine was 7 or 8. So I just stayed home.

"What I did was sleep, watch television. My mom and dad had wanted me to get home-schooled or tutored, but I didn't do it until later. It was just hard to even think about something like that—it seemed like way too much effort at first."

Video games, television, and homework kept Daniel occupied at home between his chemotherapy appointments.

Daniel remembers thinking that going to a basketball game might get him energized. "I've always played basketball in the winter," he says. "Always with the same bunch of guys. I'd been home for a little while, and I thought that it would be fun to go to the game—maybe I'd even get to play a little. It was fun seeing my friends and everything, but I was so tired! I went in for a little while, but it was hard even lifting up my arms to try to shoot a basket. I thought, 'OK, I'll just watch'—so that's what I did."

"IT REALLY WASN'T THAT BORING"

Daniel says that after this he was frustrated—to say the least. "Nobody likes to fail," he says. "And feeling like you're so weak, especially in front of your friends, isn't fun. But I guess nobody really cared. I'd been lying in a hospital bed or lying around at home—so I was out of shape and tired from the medicine.

"And most of the time, I could manage to do a few things during the day at home. It really wasn't that boring. Eventually I had a tutor come, and so there would be homework to do. I've always been a pretty good student, so it wasn't bad.

"And my dad bought me a Nintendo, so there was something to play with here. My friends would call or come over, and that was fun. And once in a while my mom and I would go out for a little while. Maybe go to get lunch or something. Just a change of scene from the house."

Like many people on chemo, Daniel was given a steroid to take to combat some of the side effects of the chemo. As a result, he developed the chubby cheeks and appetite surges that are common side effects of the steroid.

"We have some pictures of me back then—you'd never even know it was me, I don't think," he says smiling. "It's funny how your face seems so different when you retain water like that. And combined with my lack of hair—I really didn't look much like I do now. But was I hungry! I got to crave things like salads and pickles—salty things I never thought that much about before."

Daniel says that one of the medicine's side effects wasn't so pleasant—it made him impatient and crabby occasionally. "I'd feel frustrated or something, and I'd get mad," he says. "I don't know if it's just that I was so tired that I didn't care, or what. But I guess my family—my little brother as well as my parents—would be the targets, because they were around me the most. I tried not to let that happen too much. I knew I'd be hurting their feelings. And they were doing a lot for me, and it made it seem like I was un-grateful, you know?"

"THE SAME DAN"

Although Daniel didn't return to school full-time until well into his seventh grade year, he did visit his class a few times before then.

"I went to a small school, so it was really easy," he says. "I'd missed most of sixth grade—from that day in November when I found that lump on my neck, to the end of the year. And part of seventh grade. I know I looked different—no hair, fat cheeks. But nobody laughed or said anything. They all knew me—I was the same Dan. If I'd gone to a big junior high or something, I'm sure it would have been a lot different.

"And after that first year of chemo, I got on a lesser dose. It wasn't nearly as hard—I didn't get as sick or tired. The one thing that was hard was always being worried about catching a cold or flu or some-thing. That kind of cut down on the visitors—especially my friends. Anybody with even the sniffles couldn't get by my mom at the door!"

GOING BACK

Daniel's chemotherapy is almost finished now—and because it is mostly pills that he takes, rather than IV drips, he isn't at the hospital as often.

"I still take part in a lot of activities, though," he says. "I get invited to a lot of stuff, being kind of a graduate of that eighth floor, I guess. Sometimes it's basketball games—like someone will invite some kids to the Timberwolves game, and we'd get to use one of the suites.

"And I also go up there to the eighth floor to talk to kids who have just been diagnosed. I remember how that was, and how someone came in and talked to me. The thing is, you're supposed to just go in, spend some time, so they can see you're healthy and busy—just a normal kid. I'm in good shape, and my hair has grown back—all of that stuff. It helps a lot—I can say that from experience. So that's a good thing, and I try to go in whenever they need me."

Daniel walks slowly into the kitchen and gets more water.

"And sometimes you get to see famous people when you're up on the eighth floor. I remember seeing baseball players and Vikings players when I was there getting chemo. One time I got to talk to Robert Smith, you know the Vikings running back?

"He's so nice! It's as though he's really interested when he talks to you. He isn't just doing it, you know, to get his picture taken or

Daniel says it was easy to return to his small school even though he looked different. "They all knew me," he says, "I was the same Dan."

anything. And sometimes football players are made to seem as though they aren't smart, but Robert Smith is really, really smart. He told me that he's thinking of becoming a doctor when he's through with football. He majored in some kind of science in college, so it probably wouldn't be that hard for him to switch over."

DIFFERENT FEELINGS

There are some times, Daniel admits, that he would rather not think about the hospital or take part in certain activities. "I'll get an invitation for something, and I'll think, 'I don't know too many of those kids.' Or maybe I don't want to be reminded of cancer right now, you know? It isn't like I'm forgetting about it really, but I just feel like being a healthy kid right now, instead of a kid who had cancer. And hanging around my healthy friends seems more real to me at times.

"There are ways, though, that having had cancer has really changed me. I think it's made me act older—kind of more adult, I guess you'd say. Maybe it was that I was around adults most of the time—instead of hanging around with my friends at school for sixth grade and part of seventh, I was hanging around with my doctor and a bunch of nurses and my parents. I saw my friends sometimes, but not nearly as often as I had when I was healthy."

Daniel says that people have asked him how he can seem so positive and optimistic. He confides that although he might have seemed that way, it was often just a front for other feelings.

"Really," he says, "I did feel scared sometimes. But you know, Dr. Bendel and the other doctors were working hard for me, and Lee, my best nurse. And I knew that the kids at school and my relatives were praying for me. And my mom—she was relentless! She'd say, 'You just gotta get through this, Daniel. Just get through this, don't think about it.' I'd hear that when I'd be sick and throwing up and tired. But she was right—I did get through it."

"WE'RE SO PROUD OF HIM"

The phone has rung again, and Sandy tells Daniel to answer it.

"They're going to keep calling, otherwise," she says. "Just make your plans and get it over with."

Although she pretends to be perturbed with his active social life, Sandy takes obvious delight in the fact that he feels so well. "He was so sick," she says. "And to see him now, you'd never know it. We were so shocked by the diagnosis—I know Daniel didn't realize how shocked we were. Really, I was thinking mono or something. But to be told your child has cancer really puts a new spin on things.

"Like he said, cancer used to be this horrible thing—a death sentence. And that's precisely the feeling we had—it's just my generation's instinctive reaction to the word, I guess. It was just assumed when we were young that someone with cancer couldn't get well. But now, it's a whole new attitude. It's a battle the doctors are winning."

Sandy looks a little embarrassed. "I know I get going on this topic, but it's become so important to me. We've been allowed to be optimistic because of the great doctors and nurses. And seeing Daniel go from being so sick to being able to rally and get above it, that was really gratifying. That positive attitude that Dr. Bendel and the staff had was so helpful."

She smiles as Daniel skids across the floor in his stocking feet.

"Got everything figured out?" she asks.

LOOKING DOWN THE ROAD

Daniel remembers something he'd been ready to say earlier but got sidetracked. "One other thing I got out of having cancer was an idea of what I'm going to do when I grow up," he says. "I've talked to Dr. Bendel about it, too. I want to be a doctor—work with cancer patients. Or maybe do research; I'm not sure.

"One thing she told me was that I'd actually have very easy access to medical school because I'd had cancer! That seemed surprising to me. But I guess their reasoning is I'd be able to understand how people are feeling or what they're worrying about, since I've gone through it myself. Life experience, I guess. I'd never really thought about being a doctor before, but now I'm pretty sure it's what I want to be.

Daniel has resumed most of the activities he was involved in before he got cancer.

"I haven't had biology yet in high school—usually that's sophomore year—and I'm just a freshman. I'm good in physical science, though. Most of my classes have been good so far—I really like high school. I'm busier than I've been in a long time—there's no way I could have done all this stuff two years ago!

"I played football this fall, and I made the A team for basketball—for the freshman team. That was pretty exciting, because I'm not back to where I used to be yet. Sports are easier than they were back a couple of years ago, but it's mostly the endurance. I can run

Having regained his strength, Daniel is able to enjoy sports like snowboarding and football again.

fast and my shot is back, but I can't keep the pace up for a whole game yet."

No Limits

Daniel says he's not sure how many people know about his cancer—after all, he's in a bigger school now. "I think word has gotten around." He shrugs. "So far, people haven't treated me any different. I haven't noticed it, anyway. But I'm still on chemo—just until next month, anyway. It's not like I'm ashamed of it or anything.

"I'm glad that I haven't really had to limit my activities. That would be hard, starting high school and not being able to do things, try out for things. Like I'm hoping my parents will let me try out for lacrosse this spring."

He looks pointedly at his mother, who merely smiles back at him. Daniel sighs, acting greatly misunderstood.

"And if not, I'll just take a little time off before all the summer stuff kicks in, like baseball and that. I'm going to take a weightlifting course this spring. I guess there's just a lot of new things, and it's kind of fun to think of all the possibilities.

"Sports are fun, but I hang out a lot with my friends. On weekends we rent movies or just hang out. I hang out with Bobby, Jake, Devon, Kelly—a lot of kids. Some are old friends from grade school who knew me before I had cancer. And some are new friends I just made this year."

Pills, Pills, and More Pills

Will his life change dramatically when he is off this chemotherapy cycle? In some ways it will, Daniel thinks. "One thing is the end of this chest catheter," he says. "I've had it in for two years now. It'll be coming out in January—and that will be a big deal. It feels like I've always had it, like it's a permanent part of my body. Getting it taken out will feel strange, but good.

"Another thing will be the end of all the pills I'm taking. I can't even imagine all the pills I've taken over the last couple of years. Now, like I said, it's only two and a half each night before bed. But at one time I was taking so many! They really packed you down—thirteen at one sitting, breakfast, lunch, and dinner. Some were immune system builders, so I wouldn't get sick while the chemo was going. Some were the steroid, others were the chemo itself."

There will be a lot less for him and his parents to keep track of, too. "Now I have to sort of plan ahead," he explains. "Like if I'm going over to someone's house and I'm going to sleep over, I have to take my pills earlier, like at dinner. And I'm not sure if I'll think about having had cancer less without taking all that medicine—I guess I'll have to see if that will change."

FIVE YEARS

Daniel insists that he doesn't worry very much about his health. He's had good care, and he's tried to follow what his doctor has told him to do.

"What Dr. Bendel has told me is that as soon as five years have gone by—that's five years from the end of my chemo, which is next month—I will be cured. It sounds like a long time to me, because I'll be in college by then. But I think it will really go pretty fast—I'll be busy. And I'll have to go in for blood work and check-ups on a regular basis—but less and less often as time goes by."

Hearing Daniel mention college, Sandy smiles ruefully. "It's exciting for him, but it will be murder on his dad and me," she admits. "I'm not a worrier, but I kind of got into that role of protector, I guess. I made sure he got his medicine, made sure he wasn't coming into lots of contact with other kids with colds and the flu, drove him to appointments, things like that. But he's right—he'll be in charge of himself soon enough. It will be a hard thing for me to just let go."

"WE FOCUSED ON CELEBRATING"

Sandy says that early November, around the time of Daniel's birthday, has taken on a whole new significance for their family. "As I'm sure Daniel mentioned, he was diagnosed right after his birthday—on November 6. So for him, it's kind of a strange feeling, I'm sure. Not pure excitement for turning a new age, because it's tinged with all those memories.

"That first year we went out to dinner on that day, the first anniversary of his diagnosis. It seemed like such a momentous occasion, and it's been such a big part of Daniel's life, it seemed important to mark it. We focused on celebrating how well he'd been doing."

Daniel says things are different now. "Now the day kind of comes and goes, and we don't really make a big deal of it. Things are back to normal, I guess."

The phone rings again, and from somewhere in the house his brother's voice yells, "Daniel! It's for you!"

Epilogue

In the time since they were first interviewed for this book, there have been changes in the lives of the four young people. LaNé, for example, has been enjoying her school year. She went to two school dances and has a new boyfriend. She has improved her science grade, though not as much as she had hoped. Although she is healthy, she admits to an aching knee—perhaps a sign that the metal rod in her leg needs to be adjusted. In another month, she will have an important doctor's appointment, during which her doctor will take scans, to make sure she is still cancer-free.

Daniel is playing lacrosse for his high school. He feels that his energy and endurance have come a long way since we last talked. He has done well in his classes and is especially excited about starting his behind-the-wheel driving lessons. He has had his chest catheter taken out and says he was glad to see the last of it.

Kristin's news has not been as good. After her doctors let her go home in March, she had a recurrence of a tumor in her chest within a few days and had to return to the hospital. Her father says that although being told by doctors that they are running out of options, Kristin remains cheerful and optimistic.

Finally, Cullen has finished his first year of college. He has felt fine, but he recently received the news that his father was diagnosed with cancer. "At least I can identify with what he's going through," Cullen says. His father, a dentist, is back to work after an extended hospital stay, but he is trying not to overdo things. The family is close-knit and gives him all the support they can.

Ways You Can Get Involved

READERS WHO ARE INTERESTED IN FINDING OUT MORE ABOUT CANCER IN TEENS MAY CONTACT THE FOLLOWING ORGANIZATIONS:

American Cancer Society
(800) 227-2345
website: www2.cancer.org

The American Cancer Society is dedicated to eliminating cancer as a major health threat by education, advocacy, research, and service. With more than 3,400 local units nationwide, the ACS coordinates programs on a community basis. Its website provides up-to-the-minute news about new methods of detection and treatment. In addition, the society acts as a political advocate by educating policy makers about cancer and its effects on them and the families they represent.

CancerSourceKids.com
40 Tall Pine Drive
Sudbury, MA 01776
website: www.cancersourcekids.com

The mission of CancerSourceKids.com is to be a secure site where children and teens can learn about cancer and coping strategies. The site is designed for both young people with cancer and those who have siblings with cancer. The Association of Pediatric Oncologists assists with the site's information.

National Childhood Cancer Foundation
440 E. Huntington Drive
P.O. Box 60012
Arcadia, CA 91066-6012
website: www.nccf.org

The NCCF is committed to reducing the devastating impact of cancer on infants, children, and teens by supporting clinical and laboratory research on cancer causes, treatments, and cures. It also works to educate by advocating for the needs of young people with cancer and their families.

Outlook Project
UW-Madison Medical School
K4/438
600 Highland Avenue
Madison, WI 53792-4672
website: www.outlook-life.org

Supported by the pediatrics and oncology departments at the University of Wisconsin Medical School, Outlook is an interactive web-based information system designed for survivors of childhood and teen cancer and their families. Included on the Outlook Project site is information on financial and insurance issues, school and job issues, as well as personal stories by young cancer survivors.

For Further Reading

Elena Dorfman, *The C-Word: Teenagers and Their Families Living with Cancer.* Portland, OR: New Sage Press, 1994. Good variety of stories, and helpful bibliography.

Karen Gravelle and Betram John, *Teenagers Face to Face with Cancer.* New York: Julian Messner, 1986. Stories of fifteen teens fighting various types of cancer; well written.

Carol Simonides, *I'll Never Walk Alone: The Inspiring Story of a Teenager's Struggle Against Cancer.* New York: Continuum, 1983. Though some material is outdated, such as the statistics for recovery, this book shows how important the support of family can be to a teen fighting cancer.

Margie Strosser, "Cancer," (video). Bala Cynwyd, PA: Schessinger Video, 1994. Very well done interviews with teens fighting cancer, with doctors, and medical researchers. Good information on support systems as well as various means of curing cancers.

Index

About the Author

Gail B. Stewart is the author of more than eighty books for children and young adults. She lives in Minneapolis, Minnesota, with her husband Carl and their sons Ted, Eliott, and Flynn. When she is not writing, she spends her time reading, walking, and watching her sons play soccer.

Although she has enjoyed working on each of her books, she says that *The Other America* series has been especially gratifying. "So many of my past books have involved extensive research," she says, "but most of it has been library work—journals, magazines, books. But for these books, the main research has been very human. Spending the day with a little girl who has AIDS, or having lunch in a soup kitchen with a homeless man—these kinds of things give you insight that a library alone just can't match."

Stewart hopes that readers of this series will experience some of the same insights—perhaps even being motivated to use some of the suggestions at the end of each book to become involved with someone of the Other America.

About the Photographer

Carl Franzén is a writer/designer who enjoys using the camera to tell a story. He works out of his home in Minneapolis, where he lives with his wife, three boys, two dogs, and one cat. For lots of fun, camaraderie, and meeting interesting people, he coaches youth soccer and edits a neighborhood newsletter.